SLOCUM ANTICIPATED ONE HELL OF A SHOOT-OUT.

Every step he took was measured, calculated to make the least possible sound. Four Live Oak Boys lounged behind a barricade of cotton bales. Slocum stepped up, leveling his shotgun. Two of the Live Oak Boys went for pistols thrust into their belts. The first barrel of the shotgun discharged with an ear-splitting roar. The second hammer fell on a punk shell. The dull *click!* told Slocum he was in a world of trouble . . .

JAKE LOGAN

SLOCUM AND THE
LIVE OAK BOYS

J

JOVE BOOKS, NEW YORK

SLOCUM AND THE LIVE OAK BOYS

A Jove Book / published by arrangement with
the author

PRINTING HISTORY
Jove edition / March 1999

The Penguin Putnam Inc. World Wide Web site address is
http://www.penguinputnam.com

ISBN: 0-515-12467-2

A JOVE BOOK®
Jove Books are published by The Berkley Publishing Group,
a member of Penguin Putnam Inc.,
375 Hudson Street, New York, New York 10014.
JOVE and the "J" design
are trademarks belonging to Jove Publications, Inc.

PRINTED IN THE UNITED STATES OF AMERICA

10 9 8 7 6 5 4 3 2 1

1

"They will try to kill, I am as sure of this as I am the sun rising," the small, straight-backed man said. He pushed a shock of prematurely white hair from his high forehead and peered at John Slocum over the top of his thick, magnifying half-glasses. Pierre Devereau studied Slocum closely, as if he were one of the precious stones displayed in the dozen cases around the walls of the small shop. "This is not a lark you will go on, young man."

"I've been in New Orleans close to a month now," Slocum said. "I know the kind of people I'd be up against." His hand rested lightly on the ebony handle of his Colt Peacemaker in his cross-draw holster. Slocum usually fastened the leather thong over the hammer to keep the six-shooter in its place, but he had learned the need for a quick draw and, sometimes, even quicker feet. New Orleans was not an easy town to survive in if you lacked either a fast gun or faster wits.

"You have no idea," the Frenchman said in frustration. "Four shipments I have tried to get through, and four those pig-thieves have stolen."

"The Live Oak Boys?" Slocum knew the gang was the most ferocious in town. Mostly layabouts during the day, they became mad-dog killers when they got drunk enough—which was most every night. They lived near the docks, sleeping in the wood yards and carrying oak staves for weapons. More than one death from beating had occurred since Slocum came into town from Fort Griffin, a jump or two ahead of a tenacious marshal with a faded wanted poster carrying Slocum's likeness.

"*Oui*, yes, they are the ones," Devereau said, momentarily lapsing into his native language. He glanced around uneasily, as if this slip might somehow brand him as less than a patriotic American. He placed his long-fingered hands flat on the glass case in front of him, then leaned forward to get closer to Slocum. He thrust his face so close Slocum smelled the onions and cheese Devereau had had for supper.

"Take someone with you," Devereau said. "A friend, someone you trust."

Truth to tell, Slocum trusted few men and even fewer women, but he nodded. He had someone in mind. For Pierre Devereau he would risk much because of the small Frenchman's daughter, Claudine. She was about the prettiest filly Slocum had ever come across. Spending time with her had been the only good thing during his time in New Orleans.

"I know someone. Texas Jack Bennon."

Devereau shrugged. "I do not know him, but I know you, John Slocum. You are a good man, in spite of . . ." Devereau's gaze dropped to the worn, well-used six-gun, and then back up to lock with Slocum's sharp green eyes. "You are the man able to take care of his own business in this savage land."

"Describe what you want me to fetch, so I'll know if I really have it."

"There is no trouble with Monsieur Leclerc, my agent on the riverboat. He is trustworthy." Devereau chuckled. "With our lives we trust one another."

"If the emeralds are this valuable, even a brother might be tempted," Slocum pointed out.

Devereau gestured dramatically with his hand and shook his head. "*Non, non,* not with Leclerc. We have fought the wars together. We have saved one another from death. There are things more than jewels. This we both know."

Slocum didn't press the matter. He knew the full range of betrayal a man was capable of, but he also knew Devereau might be one of the lucky ones who had a friend who could be trusted, even to sacrificing his life. There was a quality of intensity and honesty about Devereau that appealed to Slocum.

There was the same intensity in his daughter.

"Midnight?" Slocum asked.

"Leclerc will be waiting at the docks for you. The *Delta Delight* is the ship he rides on."

"Why doesn't he come on over to your shop himself with the emeralds?" asked Slocum.

"He has urgent business down the Mississippi, and the riverboat will be here only long enough for taking on more of the wood. When he returns in a week, then we will visit." The longing in Devereau's voice for the meeting convinced Slocum there wasn't going to be a double-cross on the part of Leclerc.

"He'll know me?"

Devereau smiled and nodded briskly. "I have telegraphed him the particulars. And my daughter has also told him of you. Leclerc is like an uncle to her, as he is a brother to me."

"I get the idea," Slocum said, uncomfortable at the notion Claudine was telling anyone about her—their—personal life. Slocum left the tiny shop and stepped into the muggy New Orleans evening. Not a breath of air stirred to relieve the oppressive heat. He swiped at his forehead with his bandanna, then set off at a brisk pace down to Gallatin Street.

There might have been a more dangerous, lawless place on the face of the earth, but Slocum wasn't sure where it might be. He had wandered the Barbary Coast in the heart of San Francisco's most dangerous district and never felt the constant threat to his money and life that he did here.

Dozens of saloons and coffeehouses lined the street. Dim shapes fluttered like half-seen ghosts through the alleys, robbing and murdering with impunity. Whores and their fancy men, robbers and bouncers from the gin mills, workers from the Texas Pacific Railroad, even dockhands off riverboats plying their trade up and down the Mississippi crowded into the deadly drinking rooms.

Most of all, the stench assailed Slocum, making him wish for the open range or even a decently clean stable. A sudden noise to his right sent his hand flashing to his six-shooter. He never drew. The man in the alley was dead. Now. Standing over him was a Cyprian with a bloody knife.

"Whatsamatter, ducky?" she called. "You want wot he got?" She licked the blood off the knife she had just thrust into the man's back, then laughed crazily. Slocum hurried on. Too many of the denizens of this section of New Orleans were lunatics.

He peered into the open doors of Pretty Boy Larsen's Fireproof Dancehall, and saw the proprietor sitting in a chair near the door, a sawed-off shotgun resting in the crook of his left arm. Years before, Pretty Boy had broken his nose in a bare-knuckles fight. It had never healed straight. Four bright pink scars crisscrossed his face, and against his swarthy skin made him look like some kind of demented checkerboard. Wild eyes swung up to meet Slocum's.

"You lookin' for that whoreson Texas Jack?"

"Reckon so," Slocum said. Of the men in the French Quarter, he trusted Pretty Boy as much as he trusted any. But not to the extent of turning his back on him.

"Back room. He's fleecin' a bunch of rivermen in a game of seven-card stud."

"Much obliged," Slocum said, pushing through a knot

of men shoving each other, and getting to the next room, where a slim, darkly handsome man sat at the table, an array of cards spread in front of him. A slight smile curled the corners of Texas Jack's lips in a way that would have given him away had Slocum been sitting at the table and gambling.

The rivermen were too drunk to notice that Jack was bluffing. He raked in their money. Slocum saw one getting a bit edgy about losing yet another hand to the stranger from Texas. Without breaking stride, Slocum walked over, drew his six-gun, and slugged the riverman. He slumped to the floor, unconscious.

"We got business," he told Texas Jack. Slocum's tone caused the others at the table, drunk as they were, to stiffen. They all wanted to turn tail and run, but were afraid any movement might draw this predator's attention toward them.

"Wall, shore, Mr. Slocum. I was jist finishin' up with my new friends. Barkeep!" Texas Jack shouted. "A bottle of your finest champagne for my good friends." He dropped a twenty-dollar gold piece to the table. The tiny coin rolled around on its rim a couple times, then fell flat. None of the men stirred to reach for it.

By the time the coin vanished and the bottle of cheap champagne was on the table, the rivermen had forgotten all about Texas Jack and Slocum and any possible trouble brewing.

"You got me out of thar in good time, John. Thank you muchly," Jack said.

"Devereau wants us to pick up a shipment down at the docks," Slocum said. "Pay's good, but not as good as fleecing sailors."

"Rivermen, John, rivermen. They are downright touchy about bein' called sailors. Something to do with venereal diseases." Texas Jack laughed loudly as they made their way back onto Gallatin Street. The heat seemed even more oppressive to Slocum, although he was no longer sucking in the used smoke and fumes from cheap rotgut inside the saloon. Still, he felt a sight better having Texas Jack at his side. The man had saved his hide back in Fort Griffin after a drunk buffalo hider and his friend had taken it into their heads to smash Slocum up.

Jack was a gambler and a good one. Slocum had seen that from the start. He was also a stalwart man when lending a helping hand. For all his good nature, he was cold as ice when hot lead started flying.

"A hundred dollars, John. That's what this little excursion will cost your dear Mr. Devereau. Why, I kin jist see how high the stack of chips would be on that table back there if you hadn't pulled me away."

"Cow chips," Slocum said. "That's all you'd ever take off those men. Their pay had long since been drunk up."

"Ah, I got to them before the gentle ladies of the night," Texas Jack said. "There was plenty of money to go around."

"Whatever you say," Slocum said, tipping his head to one side and listening hard. He preferred tracking in the forest to listening for footsteps behind him on the cobblestones. Turning slightly, he glared at the footpad following them, a length of pipe in his hand. The man faded into the shadow of an alley to find other, easier prey.

Texas Jack whistled a jaunty tune as he walked, chest thrust out and thumbs tucked into the arm holes of his vest. For the life of him, he looked like a cheery sot out for a night on the town, but Slocum realized Jack walked this way to keep his hands near two knives sheathed like pistols. Not that Texas Jack wasn't also armed with several small-caliber pistols, but he preferred his knives. They were silent, and he was damned near as fast with them as Slocum was with his Colt.

The dead hider back in Fort Griffin was silent testament to just how good Jack Bennon was with a knife.

"Smell it? The ineffable aroma of the docks," Texas

Jack said, laughing. He rubbed his nose to clear it of the fish odor.

Slocum stopped and looked around, an uneasy feeling making him edgy. He had learned to listen to his sixth sense. It had kept him alive during the war—and after. The usual sounds of wood creaking, water heaving against pilings, the chitter of rats and even the sound of human commerce were all natural, usual, nothing to worry over.

This made him even more restive.

"That the proud sternwheeler transportin' our courier?" Texas Jack gestured like a Navajo, jutting his chin out rather than pointing with a finger.

"It is," Slocum said in a clipped tone. The gangplank was down and men were already straining to move the tons of firewood from the dockside wood supply needed for continuing the trip to the lower decks of the riverboat. Bright lights shone from the upper-deck windows on the fancy riverboat, and laughter drifted down, hinting at a party in progress.

Slocum and Texas Jack walked to the end of the gangplank, sidestepping the men struggling with the firewood that heated the boat's boilers. A rotund man paced nervously between the bales of cotton on the cargo deck.

"Won't be long till these fine vessels are only memories," Texas Jack said wistfully. "Danged railroads. I got fond memories of ridin' up and down the Mississippi plyin' my trade." From a vest pocket came a silver dollar. He rolled the cartwheel from one finger to the next in a dexterous move that made Slocum reconsider playing poker with Jack.

Slocum got halfway up the gangplank before the waiting man saw him. The short, plump man bustled out, wiping sweat and looking like he was running from the demons of Hell.

"Mr. Slocum, I would recognize you anywhere from my dear friend's description."

"Mr. Devereau's?"

Leclerc laughed pleasantly. "His, of course, but also dear Claudine's. She has quite an eye for detail, and her portrait of you is quite accurate."

Slocum wondered what else Claudine had said about him.

"I am anxious that Pierre receive these." Leclerc reached into his coat pocket and drew forth a folded chamois cloth. His head jerked about when Texas Jack came swinging up the gangplank.

"It's all right, Mr. Leclerc," Slocum said. "He's with me. Mr. Devereau wanted to be real sure those got to him."

"Yes, of course," Leclerc said, uneasy now that Texas Jack had joined them. He unfolded the soft sheep-hide cloth to reveal four gems each the size of Slocum's thumbnail. They shone dully in the moonlight angling down over his shoulder, but he *felt* how valuable they were.

"Takes away the breath, *non*?" Leclerc said in almost a reverent voice. "Never have I seen such fine gemstones. Pierre is the man to cut and polish them."

"Where'd you git such a treasure?" asked Jack.

"There is no blood on these stones," Leclerc said stiffly.

"Never hinted there was," Texas Jack said. "But I could enjoy a stickpin made from one of these stones. Thought I might git one fer myself."

"Buy it from Pierre," Leclerc said. "He will not cheat you."

"I—" began Texas Jack.

"You need a receipt for these?" asked Slocum, tiring of the chitchat. He hankered to get the gems to Devereau's shop and the massive safe in the back room. Too many men had passed by them on the gangplank for his liking. One of them might have seen the stones and taken a shine to them.

Worse, he might have friends in New Orleans who would hunger for them even more.

"You are trusted by Pierre—and by Claudine," Leclerc said. "What good would a piece of paper do me if anything happened to the stones?" He thrust the chamois cloth package into Slocum's hands. Slocum wasted no time tucking them away in his right coat pocket out of sight.

"Devereau said you'd be back this way in a couple weeks. I'm sure he will want to see you then," Slocum said. He saw the captain up on the Texas deck, studying the progress of the men loading wood, and knew the *Delta Delight* was within a few minutes of casting off and getting caught in the mighty river current again.

"It might be longer. I am not so sure of my time." Leclerc coughed, and it sounded as if his lungs would come out. He spat a black gob into the water. As if such weakness frightened him, he smiled weakly, turned, and hurried back onto the riverboat.

"Get on or get off," shouted a dockhand. "We're heading down to the Gulf."

Already the massive paddle wheel had begun turning, pushing the boat away from the dock. Slocum and Texas Jack scrambled off the gangplank in time to keep from getting dunked.

"Yes, sir," Texas Jack said sadly. "The days are numbered for such fine vessels."

"Let's get back to Devereau's," Slocum said. They started up the street, walking down the middle, avoiding the occasional horse-drawn carriage. But Slocum began worrying. He turned to tell Texas Jack of his concern, but the gambler was already reaching for his knives.

"I kin feel it in my bones too," he said. The two men stopped and shoved their backs together, forming a crude defense.

As if they were ghosts gathering substance, the dark shapes came at them from all directions.

"Live Oak Boys!" Slocum shouted. His six-gun spat a foot-long dagger of flame. The .44-caliber slug had already found a deadly berth in a man's belly. The wounded man grunted, grabbed his gut, and dropped to his knees. Slocum didn't waste a second shot on him. He turned his six-gun on another man, only to have the Colt knocked from his grip by a four-foot-long oak stave.

"Bash 'em good, boys," came a gruff command. "They done kilt Eddie. We kin grab the rocks after they's done fer!"

The attack had been silent before. Now the Live Oak Boys whooped and hollered like madmen as they pounded on their victims.

"Run, Jack, get out of here!" warned Slocum. He ducked and took an ax handle on his upper arm. His left arm went numb all the way to his fingertips. He spun about and kicked, connecting with a kneecap. Slocum didn't stop. He kept spinning, grabbing up his Colt, and got out from the middle of the ring of pure mean around him.

He saw Texas Jack wasn't so lucky. The man had sunk one knife into a beefy thigh. Whether his victim had swung the oak stave or another of the Live Oak Boys had done it, Slocum neither knew nor cared. Someone had bashed in Texas Jack's head, dribbling gray brains out all over the street.

Slocum fired twice more, hitting nothing. Hands grabbed for him and oak rods whirred through the air. Enough found important parts of his body to send him staggering. He heard a ripping sound, turned toward it, and fired point-blank. His bullet sank into a man's chest, but the real damage came from setting the brigand's greasy shirt on fire.

The sudden flare caused a moment's hesitation on the part of his attackers. This let Slocum stumble on his way, gasping, hunting for anywhere to turn for help. He found nothing.

"Kill him! The sonuvabitch done shot Eddie, and now he's gone'n set Sean afire!''

Heavy boots crashed onto the street as pursuit began in earnest. Slocum had a small head start, but couldn't keep going much longer. He ducked down an alley, cut across another street, and looked around frantically for any help. There was nothing. The sight of the Live Oak Boys after a victim caused people to vanish like mist in the hot morning sun.

More by luck than design, Slocum fell facedown on stairs leading to a cellar. Stunned by the impact, he lay. Behind him ran the gang, still hot for his blood. When he regained some of his senses, he slid all the way down the steps and put his back against a steel-plated door. Reloading his six-shooter, he stood on shaky feet, intending to go back after Texas Jack, though there wasn't any hope the Texas gambler might still be alive. Slocum had seen men kicked in the head by mules, but never had he seen anything that brutal.

He took one step, six-shooter in his hand, then stopped dead in his tracks. His still-numbed left hand worked across his coat. He looked down and saw that the pocket where he had put Devereau's emeralds was missing.

And so was the chamois cloth holding the gemstones.

2

"How do we know you ain't got a hand in this?" asked the New Orleans policeman, Sergeant O'Leary. He peered suspiciously at Slocum, squinting just a little. He hitched up his pants over the bulge of his beer gut, then rested his hand on the slungshot stuffed into his wide leather belt. The two cops behind their sergeant snickered.

"My friend was killed by the Live Oak Boys," Slocum said. He saw how amused the other two policemen were. He wondered if they were members of the gang—or if they had been. They were older than most of those who had swung the ax handles at him and Texas Jack, but they had the look and haughty attitude of the Live Oak Boys.

"So you say," Sergeant O'Leary said belligerently. He thrust out his chin, as if begging Slocum to take a swing at him. "A body was found floatin' facedown in the Mississippi, but that ain't overly uncommon. Happens a dozen times a month."

"More," chimed in one of his friends. Then he snickered.

"Was the body identified?" asked Pierre Devereau. The small jeweler's nervous gestures were driving Slocum to distraction. Devereau licked his lips, gestured wildly

13

with his hands, and was starting to pace to and fro in the small jewelry store.

"Never will be. Head was stove in, maybe by a paddle on one of them riverboats."

"Did you find the body down near the end of Elysian Fields Street?" Slocum read the answer in the guilty glances. The Live Oak Boys reputedly had their headquarters near the docks where the wood was loaded onto the riverboats.

"The emeralds were stolen too," Slocum said when he saw he wasn't going to get an answer from any of the coppers. "There'll be a reward for their return." He cast a quick glance at Devereau. The small man's head bobbed up and down as if it were attached to a spring.

"Yes, a reward, a good idea, a reward for the return of my stones," he said.

"The gent wants his stones back," one cop said with a chuckle.

The other laughed out loud. "Reckon if somebody done took *my* rocks, I'd want 'em back too."

Slocum considered what trouble he might end up in if he silenced the policeman. The man caught Slocum's cold glance and fell silent, nudging his friend and fingering his nightstick.

"There'll be a reward," Slocum said. Then he added, "But you don't figure anyone's going to claim it, do you?"

"Never kin tell, but I doubt it," the sergeant said. "Boys, looks to me as if we done wasted a bit of time. If we hurry, we can catch the last rat fight over on Corduroy Alley." The trio left Devereau's shop.

"They are so . . . so—" Devereau began to sputter. Slocum saw tears in the man's eyes.

"They're thieves, as bad as the Live Oak Boys," Slocum said. "I'm sorry about this, Mr. Devereau. I searched the entire area and didn't find the stones. Might have been picked up by any passerby." Slocum didn't think that was what had happened. The gang had known he and Texas Jack were coming by with the emeralds. How, he could not say. It might have been nothing more than bad luck, with one of the gang's spies seeing the transfer on the riverboat gangplank.

But Slocum's gut told him different. Texas Jack had died for no good reason other than pure cussedness on the part of his attackers. Stealing the emeralds was reason enough to get mad. Killing his friend pushed Slocum too far. Somebody was going to pay for killing Texas Jack. Maybe a whole passel of somebodies.

"The police, they will not ever come to my shop again, will they? This matter is settled in their minds?" Pierre Devereau fought to regain control.

"I'm not saying the policemen are in cahoots with the gang, but it looks like it. Maybe they're getting paid off. Maybe they run with the Live Oak Boys when they're not in uniform. Or maybe friends or family are in the gang. It doesn't matter. The stones are gone, and Texas Jack is dead."

"My poor Leclerc. This will kill him when he learns of the theft, truly it will," Devereau said, his eyes unfocused as he stared at a blank wall.

"I'll do what I can, Mr. Devereau."

"But what can you do, Mr. Slocum? You are one against so many! I have put your life in jeopardy already. It was not a good thing to do, and I apologize for this."

"They can die, one by one," Slocum said coldly. His anger turned inward and metamorphosed like a dangerous butterfly into grim determination that would never be sated until Jack's killers were dead.

"That is not necessary," Devereau said. "I must face the truth of this matter. The emeralds are gone for all time. But my other stones, the stock in this very store, this I must safeguard."

"I've heard of the Live Oak Boys and some of the other gangs robbing businesses, but not too often. They're cowards.'' Slocum closed his eyes and remembered vividly the ring of men closing in around him and Jack. One or two faces were clear, but getting men to admit to being in the gang would be hard if it meant betraying their comrades.

"Please, Mr. Slocum. Stay the night in my store. Watch over the shop. For my peace of mind, please do this for me.''

"You want me to mount a guard?''

"Stand the watch. I have a shotgun under the counter. You know how to use it.''

Slocum nodded. The last thing he wanted to do tonight was spend his time watching over the massive safe in the back room. Devereau always locked up his stock of diamonds, rubies, and emeralds there. Blowing up the safe would be hard, moving it somewhere that it might be pried open even harder.

"You will do this thing for me?''

Slocum experienced a pang of guilt over losing Devereau's emeralds. They had been entrusted to him. Even looking back at the attack, he saw no way he could have avoided losing the emeralds. That didn't ease his guilt.

"I'll stand guard until you get back here in the morning,'' Slocum said. "No more will be stolen from you tonight.''

"Thank you, thank you,'' Devereau said, pumping Slocum's hand. The small man's grip was surprisingly strong and firm. Pierre Devereau left the store mumbling to himself about his ill luck. Slocum bolted the door behind the proprietor, then fetched the sawed-off shotgun. He snorted in disgust when he saw it. He knocked open the chambers and pulled out the decaying shells.

Slocum tossed them aside. The shotgun would be more dangerous to whoever fired it than to the intended target because of the ancient shells. He replaced the shotgun and checked his trusty side arm. The Colt would see him through just about any fight.

Satisfied with this, he went into the back room, found a blanket, and stretched it out on the floor. He lay down, back against a wall and his feet pressing into the door of the safe. No one would get past him to the safe. No one. Slocum drifted off to a sleep troubled by flashing ax handles and dying friends.

A scraping sound against the back door leading to the alley brought Slocum up, six-shooter in his steady hand. For a moment he wondered if it had been a dream. Then he heard the sound of metal moving against metal. A key in the lock. Then the door opened silently on well-oiled hinges.

Slocum cocked his six-gun. The sound was like a clap of thunder in the still room.

"I'll blow your head off if you try anything," Slocum said.

"Really, John, that's most unneighborly of you," said a soft, lilting voice. The door closed and the key turned in the lock, again securing it.

Slocum fumbled with a coal oil lamp, scratched a lucifer, and got the wick ignited. The soft yellow light filling the room clearly showed his intruder.

"You could have gotten yourself plugged, Claudine," he said to Pierre Devereau's daughter.

The dark-haired woman laughed delightedly as she put a small bag down beside the door. "That was exactly what I had in mind, though not with this." She knelt beside Slocum and pushed his six-shooter aside.

Slocum felt his heart beating faster as he looked at her again. The lovely young woman might be about the most beautiful he had ever seen. Waves of midnight-black hair rippled in soft cascades over her shoulders. Her pale oval face looked up at him, her bright blue eyes touching parts of him long hidden—even from himself.

When he was with Claudine he thought of settling down, and he hadn't done that in more years than he cared to admit.

As his mind drifted, Claudine was far more direct in what she wanted. Her nimble fingers worked on his shirt and belt and buttoned jeans. She turned from them a moment to smooth out the blanket on the floor. As she went to her hands and knees, her pert behind poked up in the air. Slocum couldn't keep from running his hands under her voluminous skirts and lifting.

"Oh, John, you devil. Wait, don't stop!" she cried as he moved to take his hands off her warm thighs. She wiggled her rump and gave a toss that somehow got her skirts up out of his way.

He ran his hands slowly up the length of her legs, feeling the sleek warm flesh flow beneath his rough hands. Then he moved around her waist. His hand came to rest over the fleecy triangle of tangled fur nesting between her legs. The woman gave a sigh of sheer delight and rubbed her behind into his body.

"Your hand is so nice there, John, but it isn't all I want."

"What more could you want than this?" he teased. He pushed aside her frilly undergarments and pulled them down her legs. Then he returned to the triangle that promised paradise and ran his finger into the hot, moist spot he found there.

Claudine gasped as his finger penetrated her most intimate recess. She collapsed forward, resting her head on her crossed arms. This caused her snowy white half-moons to protrude even more into the air. Slocum felt his heart beginning to pound.

He moved behind her, both arms circling her body. He kept one finger moving gently back and forth in her well-oiled slit while his other hand sought out the twin mounds of her dangling breasts. Claudine gasped again as he found the taut pink buttons capping each of those luscious cones.

"You know what I like, John," she said in a husky

voice. "But tonight, tonight I am in need of something more."

"More than this?" he teased. He stroked over her breasts, crushing them until he felt the turgid nubs pulsating hard against his palm. The moisture within her boiled forth, betraying her real arousal.

"Yes!"

"Something like this?" he asked. Slocum's manhood jutted up, then slipped easily under her body and found the precise spot they both yearned for him to explore. His finger slipped from her inner reaches, replaced immediately by his pillar of manhood.

"That, yes, that!" she sighed.

"And this?" he asked, beginning to move his hips in a slow, powerful motion. She felt tight around him, tight and hot and exciting. It was like delving into a mine shaft. This was a place where a man could get lost and never care.

Claudine waggled her rear end a mite, then slammed back as he moved forward. This caused Slocum to sink all the way into her steamy interior. For a moment, he was paralyzed with the pleasure of the moment. She squeezed down with inner muscles, then relaxed just enough to let him escape. But he didn't stay out long.

He began moving in the age-old rhythm of a man loving a woman. They fit together like peas in a pod. She reached back between her legs and began fondling him as he slid in and out of her. Slocum wondered if the boiler on one of the Mississippi riverboats felt like this before it popped its rivets and exploded.

He moved faster, sinking deeper into her gently yielding interior until the heat and warmth conspired to rob him of his control.

"I love the way you love me, John. I love you!" Claudine called out. She began ramming her hips back to meet his every inward thrust. They strove together like a precision machine, each giving the other more pleasure than they would have thought possible.

Slocum gasped and arched his back, shoving his hips far forward, trying to sink entirely into her body just as her tight female sheath gripped down powerfully around him. They moved together until, all too soon, it was over and they lay side by side, sweaty, spent, and secure in each other's arms.

"I need your passion so much, John," she said softly. "You make me feel like a real woman."

"Can't imagine the man who wouldn't claim you feel like a real woman," Slocum said, his fingertips dancing over her exposed breasts before dipping lower. Her belly heaved as he moved lower still toward the spot he had so recently plumbed.

"That's not what I mean, and you know it. John, I—" Claudine's words of love were cut off by a bullet kicking up splinters beside her head. Instinctively, she rolled in the opposite direction, tangling with Slocum as he grabbed wildly for his gunbelt and the Colt holstered there.

A second shot came even closer, this one aimed at Slocum. He winced as the hot streak left by the slug lanced along his lower leg.

He tossed Claudine to one side, cocked his six-shooter, and opened fire, not even knowing where his attacker stood. He was rewarded with a grunt of pain, and knew his wild shot had found a target.

"There, John, there. In the front of the store! There's a pair of them!"

Slocum struggled to pull up his pants and get to the store lobby. He took a half step and fell forward to his knees. This clumsiness saved his life. The shotgun blast ripping through the air where his head had been only an instant before would have killed him on the spot.

Slocum flopped forward, bringing up his six-shooter. He squeezed off a shot at the center of a dark figure that seemed to fill half the doorway. Another grunt of pain was his reward.

"John, get back. We can hold them off in the back room!" Claudine called wisely. Slocum had trouble wiggling in retreat. Another shotgun blast ripped apart the floor beside him. A couple of the buckshot pellets caused him to recoil, but worst of all was the way he had been blinded by the muzzle flash. He had been staring directly at the spot where the shotgun flared.

"Give me the gun," Claudine said, "if you're not going to use it." He felt her grabbing for the gun, tearing it from his fingers. He was dazed and saw only dancing yellow and blue dots in front of his eyes.

"I'll be able to—" He never finished the sentence. It felt as if a railroad tie had crashed into the top of his skull. He slumped over, his Colt dropping from his nerveless fingers. All he remembered was hoping Claudine would use it on whoever had slugged him.

His nose twitched. Then Slocum choked and coughed. He thrashed about, arms flailing. When he touched something so hot it scorched his flesh, he jerked back, coming instantly to his senses. His arm was on fire. Panicky, Slocum brushed off the cinders burning at his flesh, then coughed again and almost blacked out when he raised his head into the smoke.

Falling to his belly, he choked out, "Claudine!" Wiggling around, he found the woman. He went cold inside, in spite of the heat boiling inches above his head. She was dead, a bullet smack between her breasts. Slocum grabbed at her dress and tore it as he dragged the body along the floor of the back room to the door leading into the alley.

It took him several seconds to get the door open. The doorknob was almost too hot for him until he took his shirt and used that to turn the knob. Slocum ducked instinctively when a bullet ripped past his head. He dropped flat on his belly again, spun about, and saw his trusty Colt was only responding to the intense heat in the building.

He used his shirt to pick up his six-shooter, and then continued his escape into the alley.

In the distance he heard the clanging of firebells and the loud neighing of horses pulling pumper wagons. Blinded by the smoke, gagging on the stench from burning wood and tar paper, he was only vaguely aware of hands grasping at him and pulling him to safety.

"Claudine," he got out. "Get her, get her."

"Mister, she's dead as a mackerel. Sorry 'bout that." The speaker spat and shook his head at the loss.

Slocum wiped at his eyes and saw a rough-dressed man peering down at him.

"I seen the black smoke billowin' out, and I called for the damn fire department. That's them bastards out front now, haggling over the price to put out the fire."

"Claudine?"

"Dead, mister. I tole you that." The man backed off, then vanished into the smoke. Slocum tried to call him back, but his nameless benefactor wanted to remain anonymous.

Slocum watched the jewelry store collapse in on itself when the roof timbers burned through. He shielded his face with his arm. Slocum winced as new sparks tore at his bare flesh. Swatting out the tiny fires trying to eat his flesh, Slocum found himself unable to do any more. He simply sat with his back against a brick wall ten yards down the alley behind the jewelry store.

Time went by in spurts until Pierre Devereau found him. The man knelt beside Slocum and shook him.

"Claudine, what has happened to my Claudine?" Devereau said.

"Dead. They shot her. They clubbed me, shot her."

"The safe, it was open and all the contents gone. They burned down my store. They robbed me! But they robbed me of my precious Claudine!" Devereau cried openly. Slocum couldn't think less of the man for those tears.

Tonight the Frenchman had lost everything, his emeralds, his store, his stock, and his daughter.

All because of John Slocum.

"They won't get away with this," Slocum promised. His cracked lips bled, and he tasted blood—his own. John Slocum vowed there would be other blood spilled soon, and this time it wouldn't be his.

Claudine Devereau would be avenged.

3

The Vieux Carré came alive at night like some slippery, deadly snake trying to crawl up your leg. The sounds and smells mingling with the humid summer air made Slocum light-headed with its seductive perfume. Barrel house after barrel house crowded haphazardly alongside the bagnios, and behind some of the emporia serving hideous, gut-searing liquors of homemade contrivance were rat pits. Men threw in dogs to see how many of the fierce harbor rats their hounds could slaughter—and how fast. The coppery scent of rat and dog blood wafted past Slocum as he stopped on a corner, studying the street.

The Live Oak Boys were nowhere to be seen this night. That didn't mean he would not run afoul of them. When he did, Slocum intended for it to be one on one. He knew he could take any single member of the gang. But put them together with their deadly oak cudgels, and he was certain he would end up like Texas Jack.

"Want to have a good time, mister?" called a prostitute from an upstairs window above a saloon. She leaned out, naked to the waist, her nipples painted a fiery red. The Cyprian moved her shoulders from side to side, causing her breasts to shake in what she considered a seductive manner.

When she got no response from Slocum, she made an obscene gesture and shouted, "Whatya want, a peg boy? You one of them cowboys what likes boys—or sheep?"

Slocum moved on and let the harridan proposition someone else who happened to stop under her window. The French Quarter offered anything any man could want. Sex, booze, gambling, opium. Slocum wasn't interested in any of it right now. He sought the emeralds and the other precious gems stolen from Pierre Devereau—and the men responsible for Claudine's death.

Some gut-level instinct told him that if he brought the lovely woman's killers to quick and deadly justice, he'd also remove the need to hunt any further for Texas Jack's killers and the men who had robbed Devereau of his gem-stones.

He pushed through the door of a small saloon, which was narrow and running deep into the block rather than providing a considerable amount of frontage with vulnerable windows. From the considerable number of drunks inside and the way they tossed chairs and glasses around in wild abandon, a plate-glass window didn't have any more chance of surviving than a celluloid collar in Hell.

"What'll it be?" asked the barkeep, a brawny man sporting cow-horn mustaches.

"Whiskey," Slocum said, knowing he wasn't likely to get anything that had ever seen the blush of a Kentucky dawn. The rotgut splashed into a glass in front of him had probably been concocted in the back room from grain alcohol, nitric acid, and enough chewing tobacco to add the right color. Slocum knocked it back and felt the harsh liquor burn all the way down his throat.

"Too much acid," he said.

"Got better stuff right heah. I drink it myself," the barkeep said, getting another bottle from under the bar. Slocum tried a shot of this tarantula juice. It was smoother, which meant nothing more than more grain al-

cohol and less nitric acid. He could taste the tobacco that
lent color to the witches' brew.

"Put some burned peach pit into it to kill the acid sting
a mite," the barkeep explained. He polished a glass with
a dirty rag and tipped his head to one side, studying Slocum. "I seen you in here before, ain't I?"

"Maybe," Slocum said. "Maybe not." He couldn't remember if he had happened by this particular drinking
emporium during his month in New Orleans. They all
looked pretty much the same to him. And all served the
same belly-ripping blend of a mule's kick and pure alcohol.

"Georgia," the man said. "You hail from Georgia,
don't you?"

Slocum nodded, wondering at the man's interest.

"You lookin' for some adventure?" the barkeep finally
asked when Slocum didn't answer.

"I'm always on the lookout for something different, but
right now I'm hunting for a man who owes me a wad of
money."

"Oh?"

Slocum described one member of the Live Oak Boys
that he had gotten a good look at. The barkeep shrugged
it off.

"Sounds like any of a hundred galoots what come in
here."

"Figures. He probably hightailed it rather than paying
me my due," Slocum said. He indicated he wanted another drink. The bartender quickly poured, then leaned
forward.

"You have Southern leanings?"

"I rode with Quantrill," Slocum said. This produced a
chuckle from the mustachioed barkeep.

"Who didn't?"

"I was a captain. I rode with Bloody Bill Anderson
and Little Archie and the rest for well nigh eighteen
months till I got shot." Slocum didn't bother telling the

barkeep it had been Anderson who had gutshot him after he had complained about murdering boys as young as eight during the Lawrence raid.

"You really rode with Quantrill hisself?" The barkeep seemed more impressed now. Slocum wanted information. If it took telling a bit of the truth to get it, he wasn't past doing that.

"Don't rightly care if you believe me or not," Slocum said.

The barkeep leaned even closer until Slocum could smell the whiskey on his breath. "There's a bunch a formin' that can use a man of your background."

"So?"

"So a military background would be real handy for what they're plannin'," the bartender said.

Slocum tried to hide his disgust. If the barkeep hadn't been half drunk, Slocum would have failed completely. As it was, the bartender wasn't paying attention to the scowl wrinkling Slocum's forehead. Getting a nickel in his hand for every crack-brained scheme of the South rebelling again would have made Slocum rich by now. Too many south of the Mason-Dixon Line didn't understand that they had lost the war. The carpetbaggers and Reconstruction scalawags had caused the wounds opened during the war to fester. Slocum wasn't happy the Confederacy had lost, but he accepted it.

Some didn't. Some couldn't.

"I can't go planning anything until I get some money from the gent who owes me," Slocum said. He decided to embroider on his story a little more. The barkeep obviously recognized his description of the member of the Live Oak Boys. "Truth of the matter is, I can hardly pay for the drinks." Slocum held up his hand. "Don't fret. I *can* pay. I always pay what's due."

His thoughts flashed to drawing his Colt and emptying it into the gut of whoever had killed Claudine. He *always* paid his debts, and this one was not going to be erased this side of Hell.

"My name's Lloyd," the barkeep said, thrusting out his dirty hand for Slocum to shake.

"Pleased to make your acquaintance," Slocum said. He looked around the narrow barrel house. Barrels of liquor and beer lined the walls, giving a tad of protection should lead start flying from drunkenly pointed six-shooters. From the rear came loud laughter. Slocum reckoned the cribs were back there, maybe as many as a dozen rooms hardly the size of coffins holding a bed, a whore, and her customer.

All in all, Lloyd's place was typical of Gallatin Street drinking establishments.

"You down on your luck?" asked Lloyd. "I kin use some help keepin' the fights down. You crack a head or two and I bet they'd settle down right quick."

"Maybe," Slocum said. He stepped aside as a falling body came past. The man following his victim lashed out with a wicked knife. Slocum thrust out his foot and tripped the knife-wielding brigand. A hard kick sent the knife spinning from his grip.

The man came to his knees, glaring hotly at Slocum.

"You keep out of this," came the warning. "I seen him. He's *mine*!"

"He belongs to the house," Slocum said coldly. The man on his knees turned uneasily and scuttled away, getting to his feet and leaving quickly. Slocum bent, pulled the unconscious man up, and draped him over the bar. "What do you want done with him?" he asked the barkeep.

"Out back. Past the cribs and into the alley. Them whores will pick his carcass clean." Lloyd laughed. "Hell and damnation, he'll wake up and think he had hisself a fine ole time!"

Slocum grabbed the man's collar and pulled him away from the bar. Half-clad women poked their heads out of the tiny rooms as he dragged the drunk past. Slocum heaved him into the alley to lie moaning in a pile of garbage. Already he saw shadowy figures moving closer, ready to steal money and boots and anything else worth taking.

Slocum hoped they left the man his life. He went back into Lloyd's saloon.

"Look at 'em," Lloyd chortled. "Already these naughty gents is quietin' down—and all because of you. I kin pay you twenty dollars a night and all you kin drink to be my bouncer. I ain't had a good one for close to a month now."

"What happened to him?" Slocum asked. He was sorry he showed so much interest. Lloyd launched into a graphic description of how the former bouncer had had his throat cut and how the blood had spewed everywhere and how it had put a real damper on business for two or three nights until the blood dried.

Slocum let him run down, then asked, "What do you expect from me for this money?"

"Oh, let the boys have their fun. They can pound on one another all they want. Even let 'em kill each other, but don't let 'em bust up the furniture. You know, them chairs cost five dollars each! Imagine that."

"I can do that," Slocum said.

"Then set yourself up there on the chair of honor," Lloyd said, pointing to a chair perched atop a barrel. "You got your own scattergun or you want to use one of mine?"

"Yours," Slocum decided. He climbed to the top of the precarious roost, placed Lloyd's shotgun on a ledge next to him, and sat back to watch the ebb and flow of patrons. Slocum kept a keen eye out for any of the Live Oak Boys, but none of them put in an appearance.

After a couple hours on the job, Slocum noticed a tall, heavily muscled man who seemed to have no neck talking to Lloyd. The man's ears seemed to flow right down into his shoulders, giving him an immobile look. When he turned his entire body to stare at Slocum, a cold shiver ran up Slocum's spine. He had seen dead eyes before, always in a stone killer.

This man was the granddaddy of all such killers.

Lloyd passed over a bottle. The man ambled over and stood in front of Slocum.

"Interest you in a drink?"

"Why not? This is thirsty work," Slocum said. He didn't budge from his chair. The scattergun lay near his free hand, but Slocum wasn't sure even both barrels fired point-blank would do much more than irritate this leathery block of a man.

"My friend yonder says you rode with Quantrill."

"Word gets around fast," Slocum said.

"You know the James boys?"

"Not well," Slocum said. "They were wild ones and preferred their own kin over the rest of us." From the man's expression, this satisfied him as to Slocum's bona fides.

" 'Scuse me a minute," Slocum said, jumping down from his perch. He hurried over to where one patron had whipped out a knife on another. Ignoring the man with the knife, Slocum went after his intended victim. The man had hefted a chair. Slocum knocked it from his hands and shoved him back against a wall.

"Leave the furniture on the floor where it belongs."

"You cain't do this—" the man started. Slocum swung with all his strength, and it was barely enough. His fist buried to his wrist in the man's iron-muscled belly. For a ghastly instant, Slocum worried he hadn't hit the man hard enough. Then he felt the guts give under his punch and the man folded like a bad poker hand.

Slocum grabbed him as he fell and dragged him to the front door. He heaved and sent the man reeling into Gallatin Street. It seemed he would be safer out front than in the alley where the shadow vultures waited for fresh prey.

"I was gonna cut him. You had no call to—"

Slocum didn't let the other combatant get any further. He swung and clipped the man on the chin, instantly regretting his impetuousness. Pain lanced all the way down Slocum's arm to his shoulder from the impact. But the fight went out of the man as he staggered back.

He seemed to consider going for the other knife sheathed at his belt, then rubbed his sore jaw when he saw Slocum was ready to throw down on him if he moved a muscle.

"No offense," the knife-wielding patron said, slipping past Slocum and into the night.

"Good work, John," Lloyd called from behind the bar. Slocum saw the barkeep had a second shotgun out. He put it back into its rack when it was obvious no one else was threatening to break up the furniture.

"You handle yourself real good," the bullet-headed man said, nodding in approval. His entire upper body moved when he tried to nod. "For once Lloyd is right. We can use a man like you."

"We?" asked Slocum.

"A band of patriots," the man said in a lower voice. "A company of patriots who are going to recapture the glory that was the South!"

Slocum started to push the man aside. Out in the street he saw two men swaggering along. One was the cutthroat he had fought before Texas Jack was killed. The other might have been his partner in the killing and theft. Both carried oak staves, the symbol of power wielded by the Live Oak Boys.

As fast as the two came into sight, they vanished.

"What is it? Federals?" asked the man anxiously.

"Nothing," Slocum said, realizing there was no way he could track the pair in the sudden rush of people from a gin mill across the street. A donnybrook had spilled out and was drawing spectators like flies to a fresh cow flop.

"You move real good," the man went on. "I can be-

lieve you have military training." He lowered his voice
and looked around, as if someone might overhear what he
intended to say to Slocum. "We're planning a filibuster."

"Like Walker down in Nicaragua?" Slocum laughed
disdainfully. That attempt to overthrow a sovereign gov-
ernment had ended with William Walker being taken out
and shot by a firing squad.

"My principal was there with Walker," the man said.
"He got away."

"You intend to whip up a vigilante group among these
drunks?" Slocum indicated the narrow barroom with a
sweep of his arm. Two poorly dressed men were passed
out across a back table and a pickpocket was worrying at
their meager belongings, taking rings and key chains and
what little money they had left. Several others, looking as
if better days had passed them by long years before,
played a game of poker according to no rules Slocum had
ever seen. They were all too besotted by Lloyd's potent
liquor to ever notice. And toward the rear of the barrel
house a man needing a shave and a bath haggled with one
of the whores over her price. As far as Slocum could tell,
the price was a dime more than the man wanted to pay.

"We can use them," the bullet-headed man said off-
handedly, "for cannon fodder. But we need trained men
like you for leadership positions. We will take New Orleans back from the blue-bellies and establish a new Confederacy, a new capital to be proud of, and then we will
give the South a rallying point for new hope!"

Slocum tried to concentrate on what the no-necked man
was saying and yet look past into the street to find what
had happened to the Live Oak Boys. He couldn't do both
at the same time, and the man intended to buttonhole him
on this.

"The Federals are more powerful than ever," Slocum
pointed out. "We couldn't beat 'em before. Why now?"

"Leadership. Jeff Davis wasn't the man for the task.
He chose poorly who he put in command of his army."

"Lee was as good as they got," Slocum said.

"I'm not sayin' he wasn't," the man said hastily. "We got better now. With men like you joinin' up, we'll have even better."

Slocum was ready to brush the man off as a crackpot when the small knot of Live Oak Boys bulled their way into the saloon.

"Bullock!" called the gang member Slocum remembered attacking him and stealing Devereau's emeralds. "How the hell are ya!" Drunkenly stumbling up, the Live Oak Boy threw his arm around the shoulders of the man trying to convince Slocum to join a vigilante army and pry New Orleans loose from the Union.

All of a sudden, Slocum took more interest in the crazy notion of a filibuster.

4

"Why don't you gents let me buy you a bottle?" Slocum asked. He knew Lloyd would not object to furnishing a free bottle or two if it meant the Live Oak Boys wouldn't bust up the place. They extorted their whiskey from every barrel house and dance hall along Gallatin Street. This place was no exception.

"You got the heart of a saint, you do," the burly Live Oak Boy who seemed to be the leader said in a drunken slur. He guided the man he had called Bullock toward a table. Four cowboys jumped to their feet and vacated the table when the gang members approached. Slocum found himself glancing over his shoulder in the direction of the chair perched on the beer barrel. He wondered if he could reach the sawed-off scattergun there should it become necessary.

The Live Oak Boys were already drunker than lords. Slocum wondered why the big one didn't recognize him as having carried the emeralds, then decided he was too drunk to do more than break wind and fall over in a stupor.

"Friends of yours, Bullock?" Slocum asked of the man, who appeared uncomfortable with the attention the Live Oak Boys lavished on him. Slocum wondered if Bullock had intentionally not mentioned his own name. If so, that artifice was long past and replaced by outright aggravation at the Live Oak Boys.

"What we were talking about," Bullock said, distracted. "They'll prove real useful."

"Reckon they might," Slocum said, recollecting that Bullock had mentioned recruiting cannon fodder. Lloyd handed him two bottles of the most potent rotgut he had concocted. Slocum wondered if even this was enough to get the Live Oak Boys to pass out. They were drunks and practiced their vice every last night. They were real good at it—and doubly dangerous for all that.

"Seen you around," observed the one Live Oak Boy who seemed the leader of this group. He squinted at Slocum, his tiny brain fighting to find the time and place where their paths had crossed. Slocum knew this wasn't time to go to ground and play it safe. His green eyes locked challengingly on the bloodshot ones staring at him.

"Here, probably," Slocum said, lying easily. "I'm Lloyd's bouncer."

"Yeah, thass where," the gang leader said, as if all the troubles in his world had been solved with that simple explanation.

"Bullock here was just telling me about you boys and your exploits," Slocum said, dropping into a chair across from the three Live Oak Boys. From the corner of his eye he saw Bullock tense. "My name's Slocum." He shoved out his hand and found it engulfed in the gang leader's huge ham of a paw.

"Street," the Live Oak Boy said, squeezing down hard. Slocum was ready for him. He hadn't spent years on the range punching cattle for nothing. He gave as good as he got, the tendons standing out on his arm as he applied pressure ounce for ounce matching Street's. Slocum couldn't gain the upper hand, but neither could Street.

"Yeah, they call him One-way Street, 'cuz that's where

most of his enemies end up," chimed in another of the Live Oak Boys.

"*All* of 'em," Street corrected. "I kill every last one of the sons o' bitches." But the man backed off on the test of strength against Slocum. For a moment Slocum thought the effort to break his hand had sobered Street enough for him to remember where he had seen him before. But the Live Oak Boy said nothing as he reached for the bottle. He pulled the cork out with his teeth and spat it high into the air, then upended the bottle. Slocum wondered if Street even stopped to breathe from the way the liquor vanished down his gullet.

Any normal man would have been dead on the floor and drawing flies from drinking so much of that pure poison so fast. Not Street. He belched loudly, then tossed aside the empty bottle.

"Good. Gimme the other one."

Slocum noticed that none of the gang accompanying Street objected. But this time Street took it easier, knocking back only a small slug of whiskey. Slocum gestured for another bottle.

For a moment, Slocum thought Street was going to reach across the table and throttle him. Slocum pulled out the cork from the new bottle and started to upend it the way the gang member had, then stopped and set it down.

"You're too much of a drinker for me, Street," Slocum said. "Besides, I'm working."

Street bellowed a roar of triumph. Slocum saw how Street hated losing any contest, no matter how trivial. He also saw Lloyd heave a sigh of relief that his new bouncer had given in to the bully. The way Bullock stared at them told Slocum that, for all his talk, the no-necked, bullet-headed man wasn't feeling too secure around the Live Oak Boys. The filibuster might be forming, but the Live Oak Boys were a dangerous, out-of-control part of it.

Slocum figured he had nothing to lose. "You boys look

to have the entire Vieux Carré in the palm of your hand,"
he said.

"All New Orleans, mister," bragged another. Street
waved him silent.

"Nobody farts in this town what we know about it,"
said Street.

"I'm sure," Slocum said. "A dude approached me earlier tonight about buying some precious stones."

"What?" Street's eyes unfocused a moment, then came
into crystal clarity. "What you goin' on about?"

"Buying diamonds, rubies, emeralds," Slocum said.
"He's offering big money." There was nothing subtle
about how he went after the information he needed, but
these weren't subtle men. If he danced around the matter
too much, they might never understand what he was saying.

A frontal assault was the only hope he had.

"Street," snapped Bullock. For once, the man's single
word caused the Live Oak Boys to fall silent.

"What's wrong?" Slocum asked innocently. "You're
looking mighty nervy about this."

"I got to go," Bullock said. He kicked back his chair,
glared at Street, and said to the Live Oak Boys, "*He*
wouldn't like it." Then he left.

"What was that all about?" Slocum asked. He watched
Street closely. Slocum was keyed up and ready to go for
his Colt the instant Street or any of his comrades showed
the least sign of getting vicious.

"He thinks he runs the big show. Bullock don't know
nothin'," Street said, slurring his words. At long last the
effect of downing an entire bottle of whiskey had worked
on him. The way he swayed in the chair told Slocum that
Street had only a few more minutes before he passed out
on the table.

"I can get big money for jewels," Slocum said. "Es-
pecially emeralds. The dude is from back East and has
more money than good sense."

"All them are like that," said Street. "Look 't M-McMullan."

"Who?" Slocum had never heard this name before.

"Don't matter. You d-deal with m-me," Street said. "How much money we talkin'?"

"How many stones you got?"

"I got more rocks than any man in the room!" bellowed Street.

"For sale," Slocum prodded.

"You got ten thousand, I got some mighty fine em-emeralds," Street said. He backhanded another of his gang when the other tried to silence him.

"I'll see about it," Slocum promised. "When and where?"

"You bring the m-money, I'll bring the em'ruls." Street belched loudly and began sliding down in his chair.

"Where?" pressed Slocum.

"End of Canal Street, down by the r-river. Dawn." And that was the last Street got out before collapsing. Slocum looked at the men with him. They were far from sober, but their leader's words had pushed them into shocked silence.

"You heard him," Slocum said. "Down by the river. Dawn."

Two of the Live Oak Boys dragged Street out. Slocum heard them arguing over whether to sober him up or just cut his throat and steal his money. After going through Street's pockets out in the middle of Gallatin and finding no money, they decided sobering him up was the proper thing to do.

"You handled them snakes jist fine, Slocum," spoke up Lloyd. "This is about the first night in a month they come in here and didn't bust up the place. You know what I pay for them chairs?"

"Five dollars apiece," Slocum said, reaching for the shotgun. He reckoned he was going to need all the firepower he could carry when he met Street later.

Lloyd started to say something, but Slocum waved to him and left, heading for Devereau's house across the street from his burned-out shop.

Slocum had expected to find Devereau in bed, but the small Frenchman was sitting up in his front room, staring into a small fire.

"What have you discovered, Mr. Slocum?"

"Might have a line on the emeralds," Slocum said. "No way of telling if the men who stole the gems also killed Claudine, though."

"It is a start. Perhaps this will be like an old shirt unraveling. A thread starts to pull out and the entire cloth falls apart soon."

"Might be. The Live Oak Boys I talked to are willing to sell the emeralds back for ten thousand dollars. Is that a fair price?"

"Fair?" laughed Devereau bitterly. "It is a fraction of their worth. Is it fair they killed Claudine?"

The way the old man spoke worried Slocum. He didn't want Pierre Devereau inviting himself along to dicker with the Live Oak Boys. Not getting a good look at the men who had attacked him in the jewelry store and actually had killed Claudine put Slocum at a disadvantage. He wasn't going to kill the Live Oak Boys and think the matter was settled. Not if Claudine's real killer still walked the New Orleans streets.

"I'm going to need some money to flash around," Slocum said.

"Ten thousand?"

"No, no, not that much. A hundred in greenbacks. The smaller the denomination the better, if you have either a fifty or a hundred to wrap around the bankroll."

"I see," Devereau said. He rose, looking for all the world like an old man now. Before, he had been spry and walked with a spring in his step. His daughter's death had robbed him of that vigor. Devereau went to a small box on a table and opened it. Slocum saw it wasn't even secured by its simple lock.

"I have only seventy dollars, but there is a twenty. Will this suit your purpose?"

"It'll have to," Slocum said, knowing that any withdrawal from a bank at this time of night would have to be illegal. He had no good idea how much money Devereau even had, so he vowed to take better care of this small wad of greenbacks than he had of the man's emeralds.

"Her killer?" Devereau asked.

"I don't know, Mr. Devereau," Slocum admitted. "I think it is a way of finding Claudine's killer, though." For a moment he wondered at the emotions fluttering on the old man's wrinkled face. Did Devereau blame Slocum for Claudine's death? Not once had he asked why she was in the store with his hired guard.

"Do what you can. How can anyone ask more of you?" Devereau returned to his chair, sank down, and stared blankly into the dancing fire in the fireplace. For Slocum the room was far too hot. The night was sultry and the added heat from the fire made the room oppressive, but not for Devereau. The darting flames gave him something to occupy his mind other than dwelling on his daughter's murder.

Without another word, Slocum left. The humid blast hitting him in the face outside was almost a relief after the blast furnace inside Devereau's home. Slocum checked the shotgun, making sure both barrels were loaded. He patted his coat pocket where he had stashed a dozen more shells for the scattergun. Then he made certain his Colt was fully loaded and ready for anything.

He anticipated one hell of a shoot-out.

Fixing the sawed-off shotgun around his right shoulder by a length of rope he found in the street allowed him to walk along without carrying the weapon in his hands. But it would take only a small shrug to get it into his grip and ready for killing.

Slocum squinted into the east. Pink fingers of dawn crept into the sky, then were hidden by rapidly billowing dark clouds. A storm might be moving in on the city. He wanted this business at an end before the heavens opened and poured down buckets of rain on his head.

Slocum left the American section of town and started down Canal, heading toward the Mississippi. He heard its sluggish sighs long before he saw it. His nose wrinkled at the stench of rotting fish washed ashore, but even over this he caught the acrid smell of tobacco wafting up from the shoreline.

Slowing, he turned off the street and made his way through a maze of warehouses. In a few he heard men stirring, moving crates and produce to load onto yet another of the endless stream of riverboats. How much longer would they have jobs? Slocum wondered. Not long. The railroad being built across Texas was about connected with the Pacific. If New Orleans didn't shift from travel on boat to travel on steel rail, it might dry up and blow away as so many cities had done already.

But Slocum could not have cared less about the prospects for industry in New Orleans. He slowed until every step he took was measured, calculated to make the least possible sound. Straining every sense, he hunted for the source of tobacco smoke.

It didn't take him long to find it. Four Live Oak Boys lounged behind a barricade of cotton bales. Two of them puffed away at cigarettes while the other two shared a bottle of whiskey.

Boldly, Slocum walked closer in the predawn darkness and whispered, "He in sight yet?"

"Naw, the lily-livered son of a bitch prob'ly won't even show. 'Nd I wanted to bash his fool head in!"

"What'd Street call him?" asked Slocum.

"Slocum," came the expected answer. Then there was

a moment of confusion. One of the smokers said, "Street didn't say nuthin'. He's dead drunk. It was—"

Pandemonium broke loose then. Slocum stepped up, leveling his shotgun. Two of the Live Oak Boys had already gone for pistols thrust into their belts. The first barrel of the shotgun discharged with an ear-splitting roar, taking out one of the gang members. The second hammer fell on a punk shell. The dull *click!* told Slocum he was in a world of trouble. Dropping the shotgun so it swung at his hip on its cord, his hand flashed for the Colt holstered on his left hip.

He drew and fired. The slug took out a second gang member. And then Slocum had to dive for cover. Hot lead clawed for his head and body. All around him pieces of cotton bale kicked high into the air.

Getting his legs under him, he sprinted for the far end of the stack of bales. This almost cost Slocum his life. Two more Live Oak Boys waited for him there. One swung his oak stave. The whistle of the hard wood stave through the air caused Slocum to duck instinctively and miss the worst of the blow. The glancing impact on the side of his head staggered him, though.

Hardly aware he did so, Slocum leveled his six-shooter and started shooting. A grunt told him he'd hit his attacker. His first attacker. The second swarmed all over him like ants finding spilled sugar.

Rolling, kicking, and twisting, Slocum got out from under the mountain of gristle and pure meanness. For an instant he had a chance, and he took it. He kicked out. His boot connected squarely with the man's chin, knocking his head back with a dull thud. The Live Oak Boy went down without uttering a sound.

Slocum's Colt hammer fell on a spent chamber. He thrust the six-gun back into its holster, knocked out the spent and punk shells from the shotgun, and reloaded in time to turn the weapon on two of the Live Oak Boys pounding down hard on him. A slug cut his arm, leaving a searing hot trail through his flesh. He never flinched. Slocum finished reloading, snapped the receiver shut, and pulled both triggers. The recoil sent him back a step—and brought down both Live Oak Boys.

Panting harshly, his heart in his throat, Slocum reloaded again, and then took a few seconds to look at the carnage he had wrought. The trap had been sprung—and the ambushers had died.

But Slocum couldn't answer the question foremost in his mind. The men idly talking had let it slip that their leader had been passed out drunk. In that condition Street wasn't likely the one who'd set this trap. Who had?

"Good-bye, you miserable mud puppy," came the words from behind him. Slocum whirled around, shotgun level and ready to fire. His eyes went wide in surprise when he saw no one there. Then he looked up to the top of the stack of cotton bales. He stared down the muzzle of an old Spencer rifle.

The .52-caliber bore looked bigger than the grinning mouth of Hell. Slocum knew he was going to die.

5

The world turned to molasses around John Slocum. He stared at the rifle pointing down at him. Every detail burned into his brain. The huge bore. The bright sighting bead. A scratch along the side of the weapon. It was almost as if Slocum could see and smell and taste every detail of his world—and was totally incapable of moving out of danger.

The barrel moved the slightest amount as the wielder's excitement at a quick kill mounted. Try as he might, Slocum was unable to get his legs to respond, to send himself sailing for cover, to even budge one inch. His senses forged ahead at full speed, leaving his body behind to die.

The rifle bucked. Slocum saw smoke rise from the muzzle. But no heavy slug ripped out his heart. The Live Oak Boy aiming the rifle stood upright in shock, yowled in pain, and finally dropped the Spencer to the ground with a loud clatter.

Not sure what had happened, Slocum stared at the rifle. The side of the chamber on the rusted rifle had blown out. He wasn't sure where the slug had gone—except that it had not gone through his body.

By now he was starting to recover from shock. The sawed-off shotgun muzzles rose and he yanked back on the twin triggers. Jerking as he did caused the heavy buck-shot to rise over the head of his target. The man who had thought to kill Slocum was as startled by the lead pellet taking off his black floppy-brimmed hat as Slocum had been staring down the rifle muzzle.

The heavy recoil of the scattergun knocked Slocum back a step. He knocked out the spent shells from the chambers and slammed in two new ones. Ready to finish what he had started, Slocum went hunting for the man who had thought to bushwhack him. Finding the would-be killer proved harder than Slocum had thought. The man had hightailed it when his rifle blew up in his hands.

After all the gunfire, the marshal and a dozen deputies would have been swarming like bees in any other city. But the New Orleans docks were too prone to gunfights for anyone to get upset over it. Slocum searched each of the Live Oak Boys he had killed for any hint where he might find Street and the emeralds. Their bodies had already been picked clean by the human vultures prowling the area.

In disgust, Slocum leaned against a cotton bale and took off his hat. He mopped sweat from his face, then took a few minutes to reload his Colt. Too much of the fight had just *happened*. Very little of it had gone the way Slocum had planned.

"Ohhh," came a low moan. "My head. I went 'nd drunk too much of that hooch."

Slocum found the man he had knocked unconscious earlier pushing his way out from under a stack of burlap sacks. Settling down, Slocum lifted the shotgun and aimed it at the man's face. When the man's bloodshot eyes opened, they went wide with fear.

"I'll pull the trigger," Slocum said in a tone that carried nothing but the promise of certain death.

"Don't kill me, mister. I was jist doin' what I was tole to do!"

"Who told you to drygulch me?"

"You Slocum?" A frightened look on the man's face warned he might become as dangerous as a cornered rat any second.

"Who sent you out to kill me?" Slocum repeated. He wanted to finish this and get on with tracking down Claudine's killer.

The man licked his lips nervously, and his eyes darted about like a trapped rat facing a terrier. For two cents Slocum would have tossed him into a pit filled with rabid dogs.

"Gus—he overheard what Street said to you at Lloyd's gin mill. We thought to waylay you, get that wad of money you'd be bringin', and, and you know, jist have a little fun." The man finished his confession lamely. Slocum wasn't buying any of it being a harmless prank.

"You were going to kill me and steal the money I brought to buy the emeralds," Slocum said.

"Don't know nuthin' 'bout no em'ruls, mister. Honest."

"You've never been honest for any five-minute stretch in your miserable life," Slocum said. He drew back the twin hammers. The loud noise as they cocked turned the Live Oak Boy pale.

"I'll do whatever you want."

"I'm sure you will. You say Street didn't have anything to do with this?"

"Gus," the man said. Sweat poured down his face, and he licked his lips in a nervous gesture. "It was all Gus's doing. He tole us we'd walk away with a hundred each."

"Gus is tall and thin, hatchet nose and a wild look in his eyes? Carries a Union-issue Spencer?" Slocum guessed, describing the man who had unsuccessfully tried to shoot him.

"That's the son of a bitch! He stole that rifle off a Yankee sergeant he kilt a couple weeks ago."

"You don't know anything about emeralds or where Street is?"

"No, nuthin'!"

"Too bad." Slocum aimed the scattergun for the man's head. "There's not going to be enough of your head left to identify at the funeral. Burn in Hell."

"Wait! I kin take you to the meetin' place. But they'll kill me if 'n they know I'm the one who showed you."

"I'll kill you if you don't," Slocum said grimly. He had come to the conclusion the man knew nothing about the emeralds or Gus's or Street's plans. He was the sort of cannon fodder Bullock had spoken of and nothing more. Looking for a few stolen dollars, even in worthless Yankee scrip, was all that drove him.

Except for a streak of pure meanness all the Live Oak Boys showed.

"This way, come on, this way, mister. It's not far."

"It's not too far between you and the gates of Hell either," Slocum pointed out as he shoved the jagged edge of the shotgun barrel into the man's spine. After that, he fell back a step to give himself plenty of room to fire if the man tried to overpower him or decided to become a rabbit. The temptation to simply end the Live Oak Boy's miserable life kept coming back to haunt Slocum.

"Claudine," he reminded himself. "This is for Claudine." That kept the man alive as they wended their way through the brightening streets of dockside New Orleans, and finally came to the end of Elysian Fields Street and the wood yards.

"Thass where we hang out," the man said, pointing into the acres of stacked wood. It provided a maze meant to confuse anyone not familiar with its twisting and turning paths.

"Show me where to find Street." Slocum knew the drunken Street had been present at the robbery of the emeralds. It might take a shotgun shell or two fired into the right parts of his body to learn all the burly man knew of Claudine's death—but Slocum was going to find out no matter how much pain and suffering he had to dispense.

"Thass a mighty big chore," the man said. Slocum saw how his captive turned slightly, his hand reaching to pass through his greasy hair. Grooming wasn't high on the man's accomplishments. Slocum's index finger drew back smoothly on the first trigger, sending buckshot into the man's belly just as the Live Oak Boys' sentry poked up his head, sighting along a rifle barrel.

The shotgun bucked, and Slocum fell back a step. The sentry's bullet went wide. Slocum didn't let him have a second shot. He cut him down with the second load of buckshot.

He heaved a deep breath, reloaded, and then plunged into the wood yard. Somewhere in there the Live Oak Boys made their headquarters. From the way the gang drank, he doubted the shotgun and rifle reports had awakened anyone. What worried him more was Gus, the man who had planned the ambush.

A slow smile came to Slocum's lips when he considered who Gus was likely to tell about the abortive robbery. Gus was more likely to find his bedroll and crawl in, not admitting he had been so inept that four of his fellows had died while trying to rob a man all alone and packing what they thought was ten thousand dollars.

Slocum made his way through the ten-foot-tall piles of wood until he found muddy tracks. A tracker of Slocum's skill easily followed them through a winding route to a surprising sight. In the center of the wood yard stood a half dozen small cabins, two with curls of smoke twisting up to the morning sky. The Live Oak Boys lived in splendor compared to what Slocum had expected.

"No sentries," he assured himself as he circled the cleared area. He moved in then, peering into each cabin in turn. Bunks stacked the gang like cordwood inside. He found Gus alone in the fourth cabin, shivering under a thin blanket in spite of the growing heat from the burning Louisiana sun.

Slocum walked over silently, gripped the bottom of the

blanket, and yanked. Gus growled like a sleepy bear and sat up.

"I'll slit yer worthless throat, you—" He gasped when he saw the shotgun poking into his face.

"I've already killed five of you worthless owlhoots. Another's not going to make no nevermind to me."

"My buddies, they're all around. All I have to do is—" Slocum slugged him with the shotgun barrel. The crunch told of bone breaking in Gus's head. Slocum didn't much care.

"I want you to tell me a few things. Who's got the emeralds?"

"Emeralds? Look, Slocum, I heard Street telling you to bring money, and I thought it was too damn good a chance to pass up."

"I saw how you searched him when you dragged him out of Lloyd's saloon," Slocum said.

"We do that to each other all the time," Gus said with a hint of pride at thieving from his friends. "Gets out of hand sometimes. Street knifed Crazy Benny last week for huntin' through his belongin's."

"I don't care if y'all slit each other's throats. What about the emeralds?"

"Street's got 'em. He's been braggin' to some of us how he and a couple others swiped 'em from some damn-fool couriers."

"Where do I find Street?" Slocum asked. He lifted his shotgun so the man could stare down its muzzle and find a good reason to tell the truth. A sudden sound from outside distracted Slocum for an instant. This was all it took for Gus to bat away the shotgun and rock back, kicking like a mule with both feet. Slocum crashed into the cabin wall, momentarily stunned.

He got the scattergun back on target and squeezed off a round at Gus, but the frightened gang member had lit out, diving through the narrow door, stumbling and hitting the ground hard. Slocum raced after him, bowling over a

Live Oak Boy yawning and stretching, coming out of another cabin to see what the ruckus was.

Slocum got off another shot, this time at the man who had picked up an ax and had set to splitting logs for a cooking fire. The *thunk!* of ax against wood had been the noise that had distracted him and let Gus escape. The woodchopper turned and fell heavily as the buckshot tore at him. Slocum vaulted the downed man and dodged through the stacks of wood, hot on Gus's heels.

The fleeing man left distinctive footprints in the soft dirt. Most of the prints were boots, but Gus was barefooted. Slocum put his head down and sprinted as hard as he could. It took him less than a minute to overtake Gus.

Reaching out, Slocum shoved hard and knocked Gus to the muddy ground. He dropped on top of the man, his knee in Gus's belly, and pointed the shotgun smack in his face.

"Ten seconds to answer," Slocum said. "Where's Street?"

"H-he's—I don't know!" Gus swallowed hard. "He passed out after he downed all that hooch you gave him. Me and the others jist thought to relieve you of some money, that's all, Slocum."

Slocum strained to hear if anyone had followed from the camp. Gunshots and death were common to the Live Oak Boys. They probably hadn't even realized an outsider had entered their domain. That was fine because it gave him the chance to learn what he needed from Gus.

"The emeralds you stole from the two couriers," Slocum said. "You and Street did the robbery, didn't you?"

"Street's got them emeralds," Gus whined. "He said he'd get a good price for them. For . . . them."

Slocum wondered what Gus was trying to say. It was almost as if Street and Gus had committed the robbery on orders from someone else.

"You rob the jewelry store that night? Did you or

Street burn it down?'' Slocum's fingers tightened on the triggers.

"I don't know about that. I heard 'bout it, but—"

Gus and Slocum had the same thought at the same time. Slocum's finger tightening on the twin triggers seemed to be the goad to fast logic. He had already discharged both barrels, one at Gus back in the cabin and the other on the run at the woodcutter.

Gus heaved as Slocum pulled back on the triggers and both hammers clicked as they fell dully on spent shells. Slocum tumbled to one side, his head slamming into a pile of logs. Stunned, he shook off the mist floating past his eyes. He saw Gus sprinting down the narrow corridor formed by the towering mounds of logs.

Slocum knocked open the shotgun, ejected the spent shells, and shoved in two more. By the time he had reloaded, Gus had vanished. Climbing to his feet, Slocum winced as pain lanced into his head. He rubbed the knot forming at his temple, then set off doggedly after Gus.

As he stalked the other man, Slocum thought hard about the tidbits he had frightened out of the Live Oak Boy. Gus and Street and a couple of others had been responsible for robbing him and killing Texas Jack. For that, Gus would pay. But the way Gus spoke, they had been hired to do the robbery. That made sense since these bruisers were more inclined to rob a drunk than plan a real robbery.

It also seemed proper to Slocum that Street and Gus had had nothing to do with burning Devereau's store and killing Claudine. That had taken more planning ability than either had shown. He had to catch Gus again and squeeze the name of their benefactor out of him.

As he wended his way through the wood, Slocum grew increasingly wary. He felt as if eyes watched him. Several times he stopped and looked around, hunting for anyone who might be on *his* trail. When he saw no one, Slocum clambered on top of a stack of logs to get a better look around. He wasn't sure who was more startled, him or Gus.

Slocum almost stumbled over the hiding Live Oak Boy cowering atop the stack of wood.

"I reloaded," he told Gus, but the thug was already on the move. Slocum stumbled along, but here his boots betrayed him. Gus moved with the speed and grace of a lumberjack during a log-rolling contest.

Slocum hefted his shotgun and fired before Gus got out of range. The pellets caught the running man on the backs of the legs and drove him facedown into the logs. Slocum caught up with him and rolled him onto his back.

Pure hatred boiled from the wounded man's eyes.

"I'll kill you, Slocum. You'll wish some damn 'gator was gnawin' on your balls before I finish with you. I—"

"Who were you working for when you stole the emeralds?"

"You were the one who got away from us," Gus said, finally piecing everything together. "You weren't buying them emeralds. You wanted to steal 'em back!"

"Who has them? Street?"

"Not him. He turned them over to—" Gus bit off his confession.

Slocum knew all the tricks, and thought this was one. Gus's eyes went wider as he stared past Slocum, as if someone had crept up from behind. Then Slocum realized Gus wasn't that cagey. Someone *had* come up behind him!

Slocum dropped to one knee and thrust the shotgun muzzle back behind him as someone swung an ax handle. The oak club missed his head, but Slocum teetered. As he struggled to regain his balance, his finger tightened on the second trigger. The scattergun roared and sent another Live Oak Boy to the promised land.

Slocum wasted no time worrying about the bully he had inadvertently killed. He swung back toward Gus, and saw the man had turned rabbit again. This time Slocum heaved the empty shotgun in a whirling circle of metal and wood stock. The shotgun bounced off one log and skipped like a stone on the water. It rebounded and hit Gus behind the knees where Slocum had already wounded him.

The Live Oak Boy threw his arms up in the air as he lost his balance and toppled from the woodpile. Slocum drew his six-shooter and went to the edge of the stack, six-shooter pointing down to cover Gus again. His caution proved unnecessary.

Gus lay on the muddy ground, his head bent at a crazy angle. He had broken his neck during the fall—and had robbed Slocum of information he needed desperately.

The Live Oak Boys might have stolen the emeralds, but they were pawns used by someone else. Had their mysterious boss been responsible for Claudine's death? Slocum didn't know. But he would find out.

6

Battered, tired, smelling of gunpowder, Slocum dragged
back to the hotel off Queen Anne's Street where he had
stayed since coming to New Orleans. He told the clerk to
get him a tub of hot water, then spent an hour soaking
until the aches and pains started to fade. Then he dropped
onto his bed and went to sleep with the sounds of commerce bustling up and down the street outside his window.

The heat of the day awoke Slocum. He rolled onto his
back and stared up at the ornately plastered ceiling. His
eyes followed the endless swirls and twists as he tried to
drift back to sleep. The heat forced him to heave to his
feet and go to the French windows. He threw them open
and stepped onto the narrow balcony. Still as a graveyard,
the street under his window had emptied so men could
wait out the hottest part of the afternoon. Leaning on the
wrought-iron railing, he stared across the city, but his
mind raced far away.

Gus and Street had been responsible for Texas Jack's
death. Gus had paid. Street would. But Slocum intended
to keep the Live Oak Boy alive for a while in the hope
of getting a shot at whoever had killed Claudine Devereau. Retrieving the emeralds he and Texas Jack had lost,

along with the stones stolen from Devereau's jewelry store, weighed heavily on him too. He had not had not much success so far, and vowed to do a better job of tracking.

"Who stole the jewels? Who killed Claudine?" he asked himself. A faint whiff of wind blowing off the Mississippi River carried with it the smell of fish and floating garbage. The breeze did nothing to cool him off. Slocum wiped sweat from his face and bare torso. He might as well not have taken the bath.

Knowing he would gain nothing remaining in his room, he went inside and dressed. Settling the Colt on his left hip, Slocum headed for Devereau's house. He was worried about the old man. The way he had sat and stared at the fire the night before told Slocum more was going on in Devereau's mind than met the eye.

On his way to the man's house, Slocum stopped to eat at a small cafe. He preferred stick-to-the-ribs meat and potatoes over the fish served everywhere in New Orleans, but he was getting used to the Creole flavoring. He had even ventured to try alligator meat—once.

". . . to Old Man Devereau's house," drifted on the still air and into the cafe. Slocum perked up and looked out the window, where three New Orleans policemen stood. One twirled his long battered nightstick from a leather strap. The other two carried slungshots tucked into their broad belts. All might have been Live Oak Boys in uniform from their scarred faces and arrogant expressions. These were men used to giving commands and having them obeyed instantly—or else. And Slocum recognized them. They were the cops who had questioned him and Devereau after the fire and robbery.

"Why you badgerin' that ole fool, O'Leary?" asked one. "He's broke."

"There might be a few dollars left," said the burly sergeant with the nightstick. He laughed harshly. "I got him to pay up before. Might be I kin squeeze him a li'l tighter.''

"Push too hard on him and he might snap back," said the third cop. "I seen men who'd lost everything turn real vicious."

"Git your asses on over to Benny's Dance Hall, 'n let me shake down Devereau." O'Leary laughed harshly, and the sound carried no humor.

"You get so much as a dime and you'd better cut us in," warned the shortest of the cops.

"Git on now," said O'Leary. He swung his nightstick around in a complicated, eye-confusing spin as he sauntered off. He didn't seem to be in much of a hurry, stopping at several stores along the way.

Slocum followed half a block back, watching the policeman and how he gathered small white envelopes. It didn't take much to figure out the cop's real business. The storekeepers paid for protection. Slocum wondered if the cop acted on his own, or if he was in cahoots with the Live Oak Boys or some other gang.

It hardly mattered. The cop had contact with the New Orleans underworld and might provide a conduit to the Live Oak Boys. Slocum ducked down another street, then sped up to beat the policeman to Devereau's house. Slocum considered letting the old jeweler know he was there, then decided it might be better to simply spy on them. Although he thought it was a slim bet, worse than drawing to an inside straight, the chance existed the cop was coming on official business.

Slocum tested the rear door leading into Devereau's house and found it locked. It took him a few seconds to force the lock and slip into the cooler interior of the house. The fire Devereau had built the night before had died to ashes, and the house was now a little cooler than the sweltering summer heat outside.

Slocum hesitated just inside the back door, wondering if Devereau were even at home. Then he heard the man stirring. Seconds later came a hard rapping at the front door—the sound of a nightstick pounding against equally hard wood.

"You in there, Devereau? It's me, O'Leary. Open up!"

"I'm coming, I'm coming," grumbled Devereau, shuffling toward the door. He had been in the small bedroom toward the front of the house. He never saw Slocum press himself against the wall and slip back around out of sight.

"What do you want, Sergeant?" asked Devereau. It was obvious from his disgust that he knew the policeman.

"I'm not here to shake you down," O'Leary said. "Let me in. It won't do havin' folks wonderin' what I'm doin' here."

With ill grace, Devereau ushered the policeman to the small sitting room. Slocum pressed even harder against the wall just a couple feet from where the cop dropped his bulk into a chair. The wood creaked, and for a moment Slocum thought O'Leary's bulk would break the legs on the spindly chair.

"You ain't very sociable, Devereau," O'Leary said.

"You've taken most of my profits in protection money," complained Devereau. "Why should I have any good feeling for you?"

"Thass no way to speak to the man who kin git back yer jewels—the ones swiped from the store 'fore it got burned down."

"You know what happened? Were you the one—?" Devereau rose from his chair, hands gripping the arms so tight Slocum could see the man's knuckles turn white. His own hand went to the six-shooter holstered at his hip.

"Whoa, hold your water, old man." O'Leary held up his hand to silence Devereau. "I can find out what happened, I can indeedy. I can find out where your stones are, and who's responsible for killin' that lovely little daughter of yers."

"When?"

"Wish it could be done in a snap," O'Leary said, obviously enjoying his power. He held up a meaty hand, then snapped his fingers. "Wish it could be like that. It ain't. I'm gonna need money and lots of it to git the information."

"You can find out who killed Claudine?" Devereau fixed O'Leary with a steely stare that belied his earlier sluggish movements.

"Seems like a good chance o' that," O'Leary said. Slocum heard the taunting tone, and knew the policeman was playing with Devereau. But O'Leary just might be able to unravel the mystery. He was in a position where he could hear crooks boasting to each other—and he was hardly better than any of them himself.

"First off, we git back your diamonds. That shows we can be trusted to deal properlike. *Then* we close in and find the culprit what kilt your precious little girl."

"How much?"

"Cain't say it'll take less than a thousand dollars," O'Leary said.

Slocum wanted to show himself, but held back. He wanted to go along to see if this was a double cross, if O'Leary was only bilking Devereau of what money the jeweler had left after his personal and financial disasters.

"Very well," Devereau said, surprising Slocum. The jeweler went to the hearth and pried loose a stone. The old man looked over his shoulder. "I don't care if you know where I hide my money. This is all I have. There won't be one *sou* more after you take this."

"You won't be disappointed," O'Leary assured him. He took the thick sheaf of greenbacks Devereau handed over and leafed through them. "Good, real good. I meet with them boys at dusk. I'll be back in a couple hours with your rocks."

"What do you get out of this?" asked Devereau. Slocum realized the jeweler wasn't so caught up in learning who had killed Claudine that all common sense had fled.

"You might not get *all* them fancy stones back. Jist

most of 'em.'' O'Leary didn't ask if that was all right with Devereau, and Devereau did not make any comment. O'Leary stuffed the bankroll into the front of his uniform jacket and left.

Slocum went out the back way, hurrying around the block in time to see O'Leary heading for the docks. There was no reason to tell Devereau he had been eavesdropping. Better to simply be there and follow whoever passed the stones along to the policeman. Slocum found himself reaching over to touch the butt of his six-gun more than once. He wished he still had the scattergun, but he had left it in the wood yard after the brutal battles against the Live Oak Boys. It had been too badly banged up to be trustworthy.

Steam whistles warned of the nearness of the river. A stately riverboat whup-whup-whupped its way upriver, churning at the muddy water in the Mississippi. If Slocum had any sense he'd be on one of those boats going north.

He had some justice to serve out first.

Twilight hid much of the street leading into the warehouse district at the foot of Canal, but O'Leary didn't slow down. He turned back, looked around as if to see if anyone followed, then hastened to a coffeehouse at the corner of Canal and St. Charles. Slocum stayed in the shadows watching. O'Leary seemed more nervous than before. The policeman spun about, his hand going to the nightstick handle and bringing it up when a small mouse of a man scuttled up to him.

O'Leary seemed about to whack him and send him on his way, but the small man cowered and said something Slocum couldn't hear. O'Leary took a deep breath, spoke another minute with the man and then started walking briskly toward the south, following the levee. Avoiding the small man, who undoubtedly acted as a lookout, Slocum caught up with O'Leary in time to see the man turn suddenly to the north and head for the St. Louis Cathedral.

Slocum knew O'Leary wasn't going for vespers when

he avoided the open doors of the church and veered to the right, going into the cemetery. Crossing the broad grassy square in front of the tall-spired church, Slocum got to the wrought-iron cemetery gates in time to see O'Leary vanish between the aboveground sepulchers. Something caused Slocum to stop and cock his head to one side, listening hard. Cemeteries in New Orleans were works of art with marble and granite tombs. Digging down more than a foot or two was impossible due to the high water table.

Graveyards always gave him an uneasy feeling, but this one caused the hairs on the back of his neck to rise. Slocum didn't believe in ghosts, but he did believe in ambushes. This had the feel of one, and O'Leary was walking straight into it.

Cutting along outside the cemetery, paralleling the course O'Leary was taking, Slocum hunted for signs he was right. He finally jumped the fence and made his way toward O'Leary. Flopping to his belly, he stared at the copper. O'Leary paced back and forth like a caged animal, his nightstick swacking hard into the palm of his hand with every flip around the end of the leather strap.

Slocum tried to melt into the ground when he heard footsteps coming up a gravel path from the north. He wasn't able to make out the faces of the two who joined O'Leary, but one was obviously a woman from the way she walked.

"Took yer sweet time gettin' here," O'Leary complained.

"Business demanded our presence elsewhere," said her cultured, soft voice.

"Business is what we're about," O'Leary almost whined. "You got the goods?"

"Do you have the money?"

"Show me the stones," O'Leary demanded.

The woman set a lantern on a stone bench and lit it. In the flare of the lucifer and the bright yellow glow of the wick, Slocum got a good look at her face. She was beautiful, but what startled him were her eyes. One was blue and the other sea green.

"Here's the merchandise," her companion said, reaching into his pocket and drawing forth a small package. The man's face was in shadow, his hat brim pulled down low. The woman took the cloth-wrapped stones and opened it on the bench for O'Leary to examine. The diamonds shone like tiny suns, sending reflected light everywhere. Red beacons and even green came off the collection.

"Lovely, they are," O'Leary said.

Slocum tensed at the way the policeman said that. Neither the man nor the woman with him caught the tone that promised nothing but treachery.

"The money, sir."

"Wall, it's like this," O'Leary said, turning slightly. He swung the nightstick and caught the man on the arm. A loud yelp of pain sounded and the man jumped back, cursing like a longshoreman. O'Leary poked at the woman with the end of the stick, then snatched up the gems and stuffed them into his pocket. "I don't see no reason to go sharin' my bounty with the likes of you."

"You're not gonna get by with this," the man said, nursing his arm. The woman never said a word, but Slocum caught a glimpse of her face in the lantern light. She was not frightened; she was amused.

"Yeah, yer mistake," O'Leary said. "Jist be glad I ain't tellin' the old man you was the ones what kilt his daughter."

"An unfortunate accident," the man said, "as is you double-crossin' us like this."

O'Leary snorted contemptuously and backed from the small clearing in the forest of marble tombs.

"See ya in Hell!"

"Yes, you will," the man said evenly. Slocum started to go after O'Leary, but gravel crunched, and from three sides around the cop loomed dark-clad men. One hammered at O'Leary's head with the butt of a rifle. Another grabbed for the policeman's flailing arms. The third took away the precious stones the policeman had foolishly thought to steal. The man tossed the package to the woman, who easily caught it, then turned, locked her arm with that of her companion, and left, as calm as if they were on a Sunday afternoon stroll. Holding the lantern high to light their way, they vanished in the mazes of tombs.

Slocum was caught between following them and helping O'Leary. The cop was being held by one man and beaten by the two others now. The relentless beating startled Slocum. These were not toughs picked for their brawling ability. They all worked as a team to reduce O'Leary to a bloody pulp in seconds. They did not boast or threaten as they worked.

As they worked.

That phrase rang over and over in Slocum's head as the three finished off O'Leary with amazing speed and precision.

"He got any money on 'im?" asked one.

Another dropped to rip open O'Leary's jacket. Devereau's money tumbled out in a sweat-soggy pile. The man searching O'Leary did not grab wildly for it. He methodically searched the unconscious policeman to be sure he had all the money. From the way he drew out the pants pockets and ripped off shirt pockets, Slocum guessed the searcher found more than just Devereau's money.

"That's all," said the searcher. He gathered the money, counted it, then tucked it into his own pocket. "Twelve hundred eighteen dollars."

"For the cause," said another.

"For the cause," echoed the third.

Slocum came to his knees and drew his six-shooter. He might have let the man and woman with the strangely mismatched eyes slip away with Devereau's jewels, but he couldn't let these three make off with his money also.

The gunshot startled him. One of O'Leary's attackers had drawn a derringer and fired point-blank into the cop's head, ending his miserable life once and for all.

"Hands up!" called Slocum. "I got you covered!"

He expected an instant of hesitation. Maybe he would have to cut down one of them—he intended to go for the one with Devereau's money in his pocket.

That was what Slocum had expected. What he had never dreamed of was the instant response from the trio of crooks. The one with the derringer got off an accurately aimed round that chipped stone from the mausoleum beside Slocum. The flakes of marble caused him to duck, sending his first shot wide.

Then there was no one left to shoot at. The three had melted away into the darkness as if they were ghosts. Slocum cautiously went to O'Leary's side. The man was very dead. Nowhere on the ground around him were footprints to show where the trio of killers had gone.

Slocum stood and turned slowly in a full circle, listening and looking alertly. All he heard was the soft whisper of the fetid night breeze through the cemetery. All he saw were gleaming white shrines to those who had already shuffled off their mortal coils.

He was alone with the dead.

7

Slocum backed away from O'Leary's body, then turned and walked quickly from the deathly still cemetery. Not even realizing he had been holding his breath, Slocum gasped for air when he got to the front of the huge church. He stopped in front of the cathedral and stared up at the twin spires, as if expecting some guidance as to what was going on. O'Leary had been a cheap crook, extorting money from merchants on his beat. He had come across a piece of information about Devereau's stolen property, and had seen a way to make a lot of money fast.

He had tried to double-cross the wrong man.

Who was the man in the cemetery—and who was the woman with him? They did not strike Slocum as run-of-the-mill thieves. They carried themselves with the quiet authority born of immense power and money. And the three men who had so efficiently robbed and killed O'Leary when he tried to take both jewels and money had showed determination and training far beyond a gang like the Live Oak Boys.

"Military precision," Slocum mused. He left Jackson Square and headed deeper into the Vieux Carré, going straight to Lloyd's barrel house. He was supposed to be working there as a bouncer after all. The instant he en-

65

tered the smoky saloon, Lloyd let out a whoop and pointed to him.

"See there, you hydrophobic river rats? I tole you he'd show! Now pay up, pay up!"

Money began leaving the hands of customers throughout the bar, and ended up in a big stack in front of the barkeep. Lloyd scooped it into his dirty apron, then began stuffing the greenbacks into his pockets until they bulged with his newly won wealth.

"What's going on?" asked Slocum.

"I bet them varmints you'd show up. They all said you'd hightailed it after a single night 'cuz you wasn't tough enough."

"Reckon I'm not as tough as you think," Slocum said. The expression on Lloyd's face mixed confusion and apprehension.

"You quittin'?"

Slocum started to, then bit back the words when he saw Bullock in the back corner of the narrow room. The bullet-headed, no-necked man had another prospect backed into a corner. From the way Bullock gestured, he was telling the man about the glory of being in a vigilante army. This might be the gent's only chance to become a filibusterer. Fame and fortune awaited him, if only he'd listen to Bullock's wild claims.

Bullock was a good recruiter—one who just might have found men with military training capable of reducing a crook like Sergeant O'Leary to a corpse within seconds.

Slocum changed his mind about resigning his august position as bouncer in the barrel house as he said, "I lost the scattergun you gave me. Damned thing busted, and I threw it away."

"It broke?" Lloyd's expression changed from confusion to disbelief. "Only way one of them sawed-off shotguns is gonna get busted is to fire too many shells too fast so's its barrels melt."

Slocum smiled slightly and shrugged. There was no

reason to let Lloyd know of the fierce fight with the Live Oak Boys. Slocum had gone in and gotten out with precious little information—but he had brought Gus to a crude frontier justice and had found Devereau's losses were more than simple pillaging by an out-of-control street gang.

"Here's another one. Need more shells? Sure," Lloyd hastily said, answering his own question, "course you do." He shoved a box of shells across the bar with the shotgun. Slocum hefted the weapon, and found it heavier than the one he had used the night before. It might have had a few extra inches left on the barrel, or it might just have been better constructed. As long as it let him drop a man with a single load of buckshot, he was content with it.

"Much obliged," he said. "Can I get me a bottle of hooch too?"

"Sure, but don't get too soused. I got the feeling deep in my bones this is gonna be a whale of a night."

"All the more reason to get drunk first," Slocum said, but he had no intention of drinking the fiery liquor. He spent a few minutes tying a length of rope around the shotgun so he could let it dangle down his right side as the other scattergun had done. Then he hefted the bottle and went to sit beside Bullock.

"Evening," he said, shoving the bottle to the center of the table. "We didn't finish our talk last night."

"The boys are a bit boisterous," Bullock said carefully. He looked from his mostly drunk potential recruit to Slocum. "What can I do for you, Slocum?"

Slocum figured then that Bullock wasn't as dumb as he looked. The man was relatively sober, and hadn't forgotten a name he had heard only in passing.

"Last night you spoke of a way a man might find some adventure. Life's pretty dull for me right now."

"Being a bouncer ain't the finest of professions," Bullock said.

"Not as good as being a cavalry officer. What kind of assignment are you offering?"

"Captain, you said," Bullock mused. He rubbed the top of his head and then pursed his lips. "Cain't offer you an exalted position like that. Everyone works his way up through the ranks."

"Even your general?"

"Even him," Bullock declared. He played his cards close to the vest. Slocum had hoped to lure Bullock into revealing who he recruited for.

"What experience does your general have?"

"The best. He rode with William Walker and—"

"Walker got himself executed in Nicaragua. I wouldn't say soldiering for him is much of a recommendation for anything but disaster."

"A young man learns and gets wiser," Bullock said. "That's what happened." He still refused to put a name to his leader. He took the drink Slocum poured from the bottle. The drunk on the other side of the table helped himself too. Slocum didn't care. He hadn't paid for the rotgut out of his own pocket.

"What makes it worth my time to come into your army as a private?"

"A smart man could move up through the ranks quick-like. You're smart, Slocum. You might have been a captain in the CSA, but you could be a general in our army in jig time."

"General of what army?" Slocum fixed Bullock with a steely gaze.

"General in the Grand Army of the New Confederate States of America."

"Mighty fine-sounding title," Slocum said. He wondered if this pitch convinced many men. Probably. The drunk across the table took it all in, and a blaze of ambition began shining in his eyes.

"General Slocum, yes, sir," Bullock said with gusto. "Mighty fine sound to it." He drained his glass, and let

Slocum pour another before continuing. "What time you get out of here tonight? Midnight?"

"I can leave when I want," Slocum said. "Midnight's as good a time to leave as any."

"Tonight. Meet tonight at Banks' Arcade on Magazine Street. Third floor. One A.M."

"Password?" Slocum asked, half-joking.

"You are gonna make one hell of a fine officer in the new CSA," Bullock said. He bent closer and whispered in Slocum's ear, "For the cause." Then Bullock was gone, leaving Slocum and the drunk at the table.

"Want some?" asked the drunk, clutching the mostly full bottle.

"Help yourself." Slocum left and went to his chair atop the beer keg. For Lloyd's, it was a quiet night. He only had to pistol-whip one drunk, and throw out two others intent on busting up Lloyd's precious furniture. For his work Slocum got twenty dollars and Lloyd's effusive plea to come back the next night.

"If I don't have anything better to do then, I'll be back," Slocum promised. And with that he walked out of the barrel house into the muggy New Orleans night, feeling a lightness in his step as he worked his way through the Vieux Carré toward Magazine Street. He stopped outside the three-story building where Bullock had sent him, staring up at it and wondering what its history might be. Bullet holes in the brick told of fierce battles. With whom? Against what enemy?

He walked confidently to the door, only to be stopped when two dark-clad men came from shadow to block his way.

"There's a better saloon a ways from here. At the corner of Marigny Street, where it runs into the levee. Cain't miss it."

"I was sent here."

"Oh?" asked the second man, pugnaciously shoving his face toward Slocum's. The man stood a head shorter

than Slocum's six-foot height, but he weighed about the
same. Veins stood out on the sides of his head, as if he
had held his breath until every blood vessel in his body
was about to explode.

"For the cause," Slocum said. He considered lifting
his scattergun when neither of the guards budged an inch.
Then the short man blocking his way stepped back and
opened the door.

"Welcome, soldier," the man said. "Third floor, in the
back. You can't miss it."

Slocum nodded and went in. He wanted to turn and
look back as he walked down the long corridor leading
to the rear stairs to see if the men had leveled six-shooters.
He decided to show more confidence than that. They'd
have him like ducks shot from a blind in this restricted
passage. None of the doors on either side were open or,
from all Slocum could tell with a cursory look, unlocked.
He reached the stairs and started up. This gave him his
first chance to look back down the hall.

Neither guard was in sight. He heaved a sigh of relief
and kept climbing. He intended to find answers to some
pressing questions. The shotgun and a box of shells would
help with those answers.

"You came. Good," Bullock said at the top of the
stairs. "I knew you would. You're sharp as a tack, a good
man."

"We'll see how good he is when the fun starts," said
a white-haired man dressed in dark clothing matching that
of the downstairs guards. On shoulder tabs gleamed small
eagles.

"This is Colonel Demeter," Bullock said. "He'll be in
charge of tonight's mission."

"Mission? To do what?" asked Slocum, but the colonel had already left to stride to the back of the room. He
climbed onto a crate and coughed to get the attention of
the other men in the room.

"Gentlemen, tonight we strike a blow for freedom. We

take the first step on the road that will lead to a New Confederacy, a better, stronger one, one without the spineless leaders that sold us out before!''

The men in the room cheered. Slocum went along, seeing how Bullock studied him.

"We will split into two squads of ten men each. I will command the frontal assault while the rest hang in reserve." The ersatz colonel indicated the shorter man who had stood guard on the front door. "Captain Fontaine will lend support, should it become necessary."

"What are we attacking head-on?" Slocum asked. "Excuse me, Colonel, but I just got here and missed that part."

"What are we attacking?" Colonel Demeter laughed harshly. "We attack the Yankee arsenal in one hour. For the glory of God and the New Confederacy!"

Another cheer went up, but this time Slocum did not join in. He had ridden past the arsenal on his way into New Orleans a month earlier. Ten men—or twenty—would never be able to take that post. Ever.

They huddled close together, those ten men waiting to rush the armed soldiers marching slowly back and forth in front of the arsenal on St. Anne's Street. Guards in towers at the corners of the stone wall made the weapons depository look more like a prison. Slocum counted no fewer than four armed men. He didn't doubt that many more were stationed inside the sturdy wooden gates.

He knew a suicide attack when he saw one.

"We will find positions along the street, in the gutter on this side of the street," Colonel Demeter told them in a low voice. "You will fire slowly, accurately, and kill any Yankee you see."

Slocum listened with half an ear. The attack was ludicrous. A battering ram would not get that gate open once gunfire started. Too many things didn't add up for him. Bullock had left, going with the ten men supposedly being held in reserve. It looked to Slocum as if the best trained were in the other squad led by Fontaine.

And Demeter's accent was strange. He spoke with a Spanish lilt to his voice, but not truly Spanish. He was definitely from the South. Slocum pegged him as being from Alabama or Mississippi, but the accent confused the matter.

"When do we go, Colonel?" asked one of the stupider recruits. Slocum was never in a hurry to get himself ventilated. No one else should be either.

"You hold your fire until I give the word." Demeter personally inspected each rifle given to the ten men. He took Slocum's, checked it, and tossed it back. Slocum fielded the weapon expertly, causing Demeter to look up suspiciously.

"You're used to handlin' a rifle, aren't you?"

"I've had experience," was all Slocum said.

Before Demeter could question Slocum further, a horse clopped up. Slocum's eyes widened when he saw the rider. The woman with the mismatched eyes sat easily astride a large black stallion, handling the powerful horse with contemptuous ease. Demeter rushed over and stood at her left side. She bent down and whispered to him for a moment, then straightened, wheeled her horse about, and trotted off.

Demeter drew out his pocket watch and peered at it in the dim light cast by gaslights near the arsenal. He snapped the case shut and returned to his squad.

"Five minutes, gents. Five minutes and we'll find ourselves runnin' the Yank's very own arsenal!"

Slocum watched the woman rider until she vanished into the murky night. He wiped sweat from his face using his bandanna, then decided this wasn't his fight. Holding his ground as the colonel made one last inspection, Slocum faded away when Demeter lifted his arm, then lowered it to give the order to fire.

A ragged volley ripped across the road. Slocum saw

one Federal guard stumble and go to a knee, hit in the chest. The other sentries reacted with more alacrity than he would have thought possible at this time of morning. Two dropped to their bellies and returned fire. Another in a guard tower turned his fire on them from the advantage of a twenty-foot elevation.

Slocum stepped back another pace in time to see Demeter abandon his command. Following close behind the fleeing colonel, Slocum felt a pang of guilt leaving the green recruits to their death. Then he was glad he had shown such discretion.

The arsenal gates creaked open and a crew wheeled out a Gatling gun. One man turned the crank as another fed in one magazine of cartridges after another until the metal barrels smoked in the humid night. The torrential outpouring of lead spooked the would-be soldiers. Trying to flee, they were cut down more easily.

Slocum picked up the pace when he saw Demeter mount a horse waiting for him at the end of the block. The colonel rode hard down St. Anne's Street, leaving Slocum behind. He refused to let the bogus officer escape. Demeter was his only lead to the woman who had been in the cemetery when O'Leary was murdered.

And without her, Slocum would never find the man with her. He had to be responsible for more than a simple theft. Just what, other than the death of Claudine Devereau, Slocum was not sure. Yet.

From a hundred yards ahead Slocum saw the orange tongues of flame licking from left to right—from the street opposite the arsenal and toward it. Another attack had been mounted, but this one was more coordinated. As Slocum had thought, the raw recruits were cannon fodder meant to distract the soldiers within the arsenal while the real robbery went on elsewhere.

Panting from his sprint, Slocum dropped down and peered around a pile of rubbish. The ten men in the so-called reserve squad moved with practiced ease across the street, three advancing at a time while the remainder laid down supporting fire. The Federal soldiers fell one by one under this withering fire.

At the head of the column rode Colonel Demeter, leading the real attack. Slocum looked around, and was not surprised to see Bullock mounted and trying to control his horse alongside the mysterious woman who had given Demeter his earlier orders, as if he were her bodyguard. Her horse tolerated the sharp crack of rifle fire as good as any cavalry mount. When she lifted her arm and pointed, Slocum turned to see what drew her attention.

A small gate had been breached. Coming from within the arsenal was a heavily laden wagon drawn by four straining mules. Whatever bounced around in the wagon bed had been hidden from sight by a tarp. Slocum didn't have to make many guesses as to the contents of the long, narrow cases he saw poking out from under the tarpaulin as the wagon rattled by him, driven by the man he recognized as Captain Fontaine.

"Rifles," he said aloud. "Brand-new Springfields."

The assault on the arsenal had been successful, but not in the way the ten facing the main gate had thought. Gunfire from that area died down, signaling Federal victory over their attackers. But in winning against that inept attack, the Union soldiers had lost a more important battle.

Rifles had been stolen from under their noses. The diversion had worked perfectly, as had the actual theft through this side gate.

Bullock and the woman rode past where Slocum hid. Even over the effluvium from the rubbish pile, Slocum caught the scent of the woman's jasmine perfume. It made him giddy for a moment.

Then he slipped into shadows as a patrol came from the arsenal to investigate the perimeter. Colonel Demeter and his squad had already hightailed it in the direction opposite to the one taken by the heavily laden wagon and the blue-and-green-eyed woman. Slocum reckoned the colonel and his squad would lead any pursuers on a merry chase—away from the stolen rifles.

Slocum didn't have any idea what he was going to do now other than avoid Federal patrols intent on capturing any more armed men ready to attack their secure post.

8

.

"There he is, men. Git him!" came the loud cry from down the road. Slocum started to bolt and run, then chose a different tactic. He sank down in a shallow drainage ditch mostly filled with sluggishly flowing sewage. His nose wrinkled, but he pressed himself down into the muddy bottom.

Slocum waited, but no Federal patrol passed along the road. He smiled. The sergeant in charge of the squad hunting for those who had attacked the arsenal was a clever one. He thought to spook anyone hiding nearby into running. Slocum wondered if the soldier was also a duck hunter. Send out a dog to flush the quarry, then shoot it down as the fowl took wing.

Wiggling along in the sludge was easier after Slocum dropped his rifle. It had been an old war-issue piece that might have blown up in his hand if he had fired it. When he reached a spot well away from the arsenal, Slocum poked his head up and looked around.

Two soldiers holding lanterns had finally discovered the sewage channel, and were examining the spot where he had dived into it. Wiping off some of the larger chunks clinging to his clothing, Slocum stood and started walking slowly away from the squad. If he ran, he might draw their unwanted attention.

Slocum got clean away. If wallowing like a hog in slop could be considered getting away clean.

He hiked for a spell, and finally saw an elegant fountain spewing out water near the old oak trees where duelists had met years earlier for their deadly trysts. Slocum stripped off his shirt and rinsed it out, then sloshed water on himself to get some of the stench off. It didn't work too well, but he walked away cleaner than before he'd discovered the fountain.

He sat under a tree and tried to picture the streets in his head. He hadn't spent much time in this section of town, but thought the road curled around and went through Congo Square and then farther west.

"The rifles went that way," Slocum decided. He got to his feet, checked to be sure the shotgun he had taken from Lloyd still hung at his side and had reasonably clean barrels, then set off briskly. Without a good idea where the woman might be taking the rifles, he was going on nothing but luck and a prayer.

But it was time for his luck to change.

Less than ten minutes after he had started his hunt, he heard men grunting and the creaking sounds of wood yielding. Slocum flitted through the banyans on the north side of the road to get a better view of what lay ahead. A smile curled his lips when he saw the woman astride her powerful black horse. Now the animal pawed at the ground as if it wanted to gallop. She held it expertly in place while two men struggled to get a wheel on the wagon fixed.

Repairing the broken wheel would have been easier if they had unloaded their wagon. But to have done so would have revealed the cases of rifles to anyone passing by. Even at this time of morning, chances were good someone would tramp along the road and wonder at the cargo barely hidden under the military tarps.

"Hurry, Jules, hurry," the woman said. The jasmine of her perfume caught on the faint breeze and tickled Slocum's nose again. After the dousing he had received, anything more pleasant than garbage might have caused his nostrils to flare. But this! The jasmine scent set his heart pounding.

"We almost got it," came the answer. Slocum frowned, trying to recognize the accent of the man struggling to repair the wagon wheel. It finally came to him that he didn't recognize the voice, but it had the same lilt to it as that of the man with her in the cemetery when O'Leary had been murdered. Not French, not Spanish, but something close.

"There, we got it!" came the triumphant cry.

"It will be light soon. We must hide the rifles before anyone sees them."

The two men who had fought with the balky wagon jumped into the box. Bullock and Fontaine rattled off, with the woman on her high-spirited horse prancing along beside. They set a fast pace, but Slocum had rested while spying on them, and now followed. He smiled wryly as he thought he could follow them all day without revealing himself—unless the wind shifted so he was upwind from them.

The nature of the buildings along the road changed from shotgun shacks to more elaborate houses. Slocum wasn't sure when they crossed what would be an extension of Canal Street, but the size and value of the houses grew until he realized they had entered the Garden District. It wasn't far from there that Jeff Davis had holed up after the war and had eventually died.

The cover Slocum had depended on earlier now evaporated. He stuck out as he hiked along the well-maintained road, a derelict surrounded by all the trappings of wealth. He slowed and finally stopped when the wagon turned south off the road, heading for an antebellum home with a large carriage house.

"What ya doin' heah, boy?" came the loud question. Slocum turned to see three men dressed in clean gray uniforms with sharp creases in the pants. At first he thought they were Confederate officers. Then he saw the starburst emblem on their sleeves. They were privately employed watchmen patrolling the Garden District to keep riffraff—like him—back in the French Quarter where they belonged.

"Lost my dog. He came yelping along here not ten minutes ago. You see him? A big, mangy mutt."

"We'll keep an eye peeled," promised a watchman insincerely. "You git on back to wheah you belong."

Slocum nodded and headed back toward Canal Street without saying a word. There was no way he could convince them a sewage-drenched man on foot belonged in this wealthy district. Whatever he did would have to be more carefully thought out than anything he had done up until now.

"You surely do take to the water like a fish," the clerk at Slocum's hotel had said after Slocum had asked for yet another tub of hot water.

Now Slocum glared at him as he left the hotel. He had scrubbed hard to get the stench off. He was worried that even after the third washing, his clothing would have to be burned because of the odor. Even in the Vieux Carré, he would draw attention.

He went directly to Devereau's home, wondering what he ought to tell the old man. Devereau did not know he had overheard O'Leary extorting the money, and the jeweler might not know of the police officer's death. Not for the first time, Slocum wished he had been able to grab Devereau's money from O'Leary before the three black-clad men had taken it.

Standing in front of the door, Slocum hesitated. What did he have to tell Devereau? Nothing. But he had to ask for a favor, and wanted to do it without going into details.

Slocum started to rap on the door, but it opened first.

Devereau's eyes went wide. "Mr. Slocum. I had not known you were here."

"I need a favor from you," Slocum said, wanting to make his contact as short as possible for both their sakes. He wanted to avenge Claudine, but he didn't want to reminisce about the dead woman for endless hours. Devereau had shown no inclination toward doing that—yet. But Slocum knew the signs. The shock of Claudine's death would be wearing off now, and Devereau would feel the need to keep her alive in his memory.

"I'm sorry to say I have no money for you," Devereau said. "You see, I—"

Slocum cut him off. He knew where all of Devereau's money had gone, but didn't want to let the man known he had been spying on him.

"That's not what I'm after. I need to work my way into a different social class. Do you have any contacts with people living in the Garden District?"

"The American section?" Devereau's eyebrows rose. "I have some contacts, yes, yes. They came—they came—to my humble ship for jewels. Nowhere in New Orleans, even along Royal Street, is there finer work for sale. I know some there," he finished. Devereau turned his head to one side as he peered up at Slocum. "This does have something to do with Claudine's death?"

"It's getting complicated, but I think I am on to something. It's too soon to know for sure."

"There is a party this very night. You would cut a fine figure in fancy dress. Perhaps a few diamonds, and a headlight diamond stud for a cravat."

"You have the jewelry?"

"It is my personal jewelry. Perhaps you could get a price for it and—no, I cannot part with even one piece. It reminds me of Claudine—and her sainted mother."

"I won't need money," Slocum said. He had a few hundred in his pocket, mostly from betting and judicious loans to men who had proved trustworthy. He and Texas Jack had each blown into New Orleans with considerable bankrolls from their gambling over in Texas. Slocum had enough left to pull off a deception—if he could even get in the door of any of the fine houses near the home where the rifles were hidden.

His plans were vague, but without more information that seemed prudent. He would get into the party using Pierre Devereau as a reference, then go exploring the neighborhood to ferret out the men who wanted a wagon loaded with rifles.

Their leader might just be the one who had killed Claudine. After all, Slocum had tied the Live Oak Boys and the theft of Devereau's emeralds to the man in the cemetery. The woman with him had been present at the arsenal robbery. If nothing else, Slocum stood a chance of retrieving Devereau's missing emeralds. At best, he would find Claudine's killer.

His gut told him he was going to rake in the entire jackpot on this one. First, he had to have a reason to walk into the Garden District without bringing the roving guards down on him like a pack of hunting dogs.

"Here, take this, Mr. Slocum," said Devereau. He fumbled through a stack of papers until he found a parchment envelope. "It is an invitation to a party thrown by one of my patrons. Mr. McMullan has been quite generous in what he has purchased from me. I told him these parties I do not attend, but he insisted on presenting this to me."

Slocum took the ornately engraved invitation and stared at the address. It matched that of the house where the rifles had been taken.

Slocum paused only a moment at the end of the path leading to the front door of the mansion. He had chosen not to ride his horse into the Garden District because of his battered saddle and worn gear. He didn't have enough money to hire a carriage, not after getting the fancy duds he wore now, and needed some greenbacks for flash, should the occasion present itself once he got into the party.

He wore Devereau's fancy diamonds at his wrists and in the center of his chest, holding down a silk cravat also borrowed from the jeweler. More of what he wore belonged to someone else than to him, but he had to think like the type of gent who belonged at such an elegant party.

"Sir, may I assist you?" asked a liveried servant, coming down from the broad veranda.

Slocum silently presented the invitation. The servant never showed the least surprise, handing it back, opening the knee-high gate for Slocum, then ushering him into the house's airy hallway.

Slocum felt as if he had stepped into a different world. Gone were barrel houses and the smell of spilled beer and raucous drunks and whining whores he had become accustomed to during the past month. Everything was expensive, and the people drifting about looked so genteel. Slocum wondered if the women might be ghosts. Their skin was so fair it looked like translucent bone china. Dabs of color graced their cheeks, and they batted widespread fans coyly as they exchanged witty comments with the men.

The men hovering near them seemed hardly any more real to him. Their studied laughs, their measured gestures, the way they all moved as if some hidden puppeteer pulled their strings at the same time made Slocum long for the harsh reality of the French Quarter.

He moved into the crush of the crowd in the parlor, not joining any of the conversations. Slocum listened, and tried to find some thread to follow. He had not come here to enjoy the company of the fine women or the clever double entendres of the elegantly tailored men. He took a crystal flute of champagne from a tray held by a servant, turned, and then stopped dead.

Making a grand entrance coming down the stairs was the woman he had seen riding with the stolen rifles. Gone were the dark clothes and riding boots. Replacing them was a lavishly ruffled ball gown. Dangling from her neck was a strand of diamonds and rubies that seemed to absorb all the light in the room and focus it on her lovely face.

One blue and one green eye flashed about, judging those about her and, if Slocum was able to tell, discarding them with that single glance.

"Senator, how lovely you could come," she said, extending her hand toward an older man in a morning coat. "How sweet of you to come here right away and not even stop to change into more appropriate attire."

"Miss Jessica, you are as lovely as I remember. It is good to see you again after so many years."

"I am sure we'll be seeing more of one another, Senator. Much more."

She smiled, the politician smiled, but Slocum read what the chestnut-haired woman really meant.

Jessica flitted from one group to another in the room, greeting many by name and seemingly known by all. This led Slocum to think she—or the mysterious man with her in the cemetery—might be the host for the party.

"I am at a disadvantage, sir," said her silken voice.

"You?" Slocum said, turning toward the woman. "I find that impossible to believe. Ever."

Jessica laughed easily, her eyes locked on his. "I do not know your name."

She held out her hand. Slocum kissed it, then almost staggered as her jasmine perfume filled his nostrils. If there had been any doubt concerning her identity, this removed it.

"A fine scent," he said.

"A specialty of a perfumer who lived near me in Brazil."

"In Brazil?"

"A Portuguese country in South America," she said,

as if speaking to a dolt. Slocum considered the accent of those who had been with Jessica. Not Spanish—Portuguese!

"You seem distant, sir. Am I so boring?"

"Not at all. Business thoughts intrude at the most inopportune times," Slocum said.

"Is it your business to hide your name, sir?"

Slocum introduced himself.

"So, Mr. Slocum, how is it you came to such an important party alone? Or are you escorting one of those fillies?" Jessica tapped her fan on the back of her left hand, pointing obliquely toward a small group of giggling Southern belles.

"Children," he said. "I prefer women. I came alone hoping to meet someone like you."

"So gallant. A true Southern gentleman. Oh, Arthur, how are you!" With that Jessica bustled away, eventually spending a few minutes with each of the men in the room. Slocum made small talk with others, but kept an eye on Jessica. It hardly surprised him that she also watched him intently.

It slowly came to Slocum that the men in the room were all rich and powerful—and all had distinct Southern leanings. Many complained of the carpetbaggers and scalawags that had flooded New Orleans when Reconstruction began. The bitterness, coupled with an unspoken anxiety fostered by helplessness at the loss of a way of life, fueled the conversations.

Slocum was listening to one shipping line owner going on about how difficult it was to do business with Yankees when a light touch on his arm distracted Slocum.

Jessica stood next to him, looking radiant.

"Excuse me, gentlemen," she said. "I need to speak to Mr. Slocum."

"Lucky Slocum," grumbled the shipping line owner, who then turned back to his tirade.

"He is so right, you know," Jessica said.

"That I am lucky?"

"Perhaps so. I meant dear Herbert spoke so truthfully when he said it was impossible to get business licenses."

"Perhaps he needs better luck." Slocum let Jessica guide him to the stairs. He hesitated for a moment when it was obvious she had led him away from the others.

"Lucky or not, Mr. Slocum?" she asked in a low voice. "Your choice." With that she lifted her skirts and hurried up the winding staircase. Slocum followed, wondering what he was getting himself into. At the head of the stairs he paused. Jessica stood in an open bedroom doorway toward the rear of the house. She motioned to him with her fan, then opened it and peered over the top. He had never seen anything quite as exotic as her mismatched eyes.

As he went down the hallway, he looked left and right. Doors were closed, but from behind many came low voices. Conferences of some importance went on upstairs, and he thought he was about to become privy to one.

"Close the door, John," Jessica said. She tossed her fan onto the bed and turned from him. "And do get on with unfastening these laces. They are so tight. I cannot wait to get out of this straitjacket!"

He moved closer behind her, his hands around her waist. Jessica pressed back into him, then tipped her face up. From over her shoulder Slocum kissed her perfect lips. Somehow Jessica moved in the circle of his arms and ended up facing him, though their lips never parted from the passionate kiss.

He felt her breasts crushing softly against his chest. A piece of lace at her bodice caught on the headlight diamond in his stickpin. Jessica pulled back, saw what had happened, and laughed.

"Imagine that, me stabbed by a diamond!"

"Injured?" asked Slocum. "Let me kiss your hurt and make it well."

"Is that what you call it now! I have been away from

New Orleans far too long!'' she joked. Again she kissed him, and took away his breath with her passion. The scent of her perfume, the softness of her long, lustrous hair, and the way her fingers explored his body all thrilled Slocum.

"I can't wait to get out of this dress,'' she said, gasping for breath when she again broke off the kiss. Jessica almost ripped open the front of Slocum's trousers, exposing his manhood. Her eyes widened at the sight. "So much and all for me!''

She ran her fingers up and down his length a few times. The blood pounding into his organ began to make it ache with need. Then he found himself engulfed in a sea of crinoline and lace. Jessica lifted her skirts and moved forward. Beneath all the heavy skirts and petticoats lay bare female flesh. She pressed it intimately against him, then lifted a leg and hooked it around his waist.

This pressed him into the fleecy triangle nestled so intimately between her thighs.

"You came prepared,'' he said.

"It is *so* hot,'' she said. He didn't ask what was hot. He knew. She lifted herself on tiptoe, tightened the leg around him, then lowered her body a fraction of an inch. He felt himself touch moist female flesh, then sink inch by inch into her most intimate recess.

Jessica sighed as he penetrated her. Her arms went around his neck and pulled him even closer. Their bodies mingled and merged. He smothered her with kisses, and she returned them with even more ardor. Around and around they danced, moving in a circle, locked together at the groin, their desires running away with them.

In this erotic gambol, Slocum found himself spinning about even as he levered his hips up and down. Jessica bounced around him, her leg tightening and releasing as they moved to the soundless music building in their bodies.

When she began tensing and relaxing her inner muscles, Slocum knew he would not be able to continue much longer. He stopped the slow spin and dropped to his knees. She did not release her grip around his neck with her arms, or his waist with her slender leg. Atop her, Slocum began moving faster and faster, building the sexual delight in both of them until he was unable to withstand it any longer. He spilled his seed just as Jessica let out a tiny gasp, then thrashed about beneath him.

Slocum braced himself on both arms and looked into her glazed eyes. The blue one was far brighter than the green eye, but the combination was as erotic as it was exotic.

"I've never enjoyed a waltz more," she said. Jessica pushed away from him and sat up, tucking her dress down chastely. "Wait for me. I really must see if I can teach you a South America dance. You will enjoy it even more. I promise!"

She bent over and kissed him quickly. Even more quickly, she darted from the room. Slocum sat back on the floor, wondering what was going on. Her perfume and beauty had captivated him. But she had left so suddenly. Why?

He stood and adjusted his clothes before going to the window leading onto an upstairs balcony. Looking down, he saw Jessica hurrying across the well-tended lawn in the direction of the carriage house where he thought she might have hidden the stolen rifles. A man stepped out from the darkness. Slocum went cold inside. Even at this distance he recognized the man Jessica had rushed off to meet.

She spoke intimately to Braxton Griggs, a man who had killed dozens of women and children without the least remorse.

9

"It can't be him," Slocum said under his breath. "I saw you dead, Griggs." But Slocum's eyes could not be deceiving him. Jessica and Braxton Griggs walked back toward him, and he plainly caught sight of the man's face in the bright moonlight angling down across the lawn. Although the light caused the man's eyes to sink into deep dark pits, Slocum recognized the planes and curves of Braxton Griggs's face. They were burned into Slocum's mind after all he and Griggs had been through. Jessica held the man's arm and spoke with great animation. Her words, though, were muffled by the night and sounds echoing up from the party.

The two passed under him, going into the house. Slocum settled his clothing, made sure Devereau's diamonds were all in place, then vaulted the balcony railing and landed hard on the path where Jessica and Griggs had trod seconds earlier.

He looked around to see if anyone had seen him dropping from the balcony. Sure no one had, he walked quickly to the carriage house, and swiped at a dirty window with his hand before peering in. Inside the large building, he made out three men hunched over a small table playing cards. Beside them was the wagon Slocum had seen driving away from the arsenal the night before.

His mind raced. The rifles were of no real concern to him. Who cared if a few Yankee rifles turned up missing? What mattered more to Slocum was retrieving Devereau's jewels, both the emeralds taken on the way to the shop and the diamonds stolen from the safe after Claudine had been killed.

"The stones won't be in there," Slocum decided. But where would they be hidden? Jessica would know, but he had no way of prying the information from her. His head still spun from their lovemaking in the upstairs bedroom. That had convinced him she was a dangerous foe—as well as an intriguing one. He didn't think she had recognized him except as a sexual conquest.

If she had, Slocum didn't doubt for an instant he would be dead.

If Jessica counted Griggs among her friends, she ran with cold-blooded killers.

Slocum circled the carriage house, wondering what to do next. The three inside might be the ones who had so systematically removed O'Leary from the living. He had no chance against a trio of cutthroats who worked together that well, if they were the ones.

The sound of Jessica's lilting voice caused Slocum to hunker down and hunt for a patch of shadow to hide in. Jessica had changed into riding clothes. As Jessica and Griggs had gone into the house, so did they return, arm in arm.

She opened the door and called out, "Get my carriage ready. Now! We've got to get down to the levee before midnight."

Slocum was not unduly surprised to see that Jessica was in command rather than Braxton Griggs. Griggs had come from Nathan Forrest's raiders, and rode with Quantrill's Raiders for almost a year. He had been one of the bloodiest-handed of the lot of stone killers Quantrill called soldiers. Griggs and Slocum had locked horns more than once in those eleven months. Remembering it with no fondness, Slocum reached to trace out the long scar on his leg that Griggs had left with a Bowie knife. But in that fight, Slocum had given as good as he got.

Braxton Griggs carried a four-inch scar on his belly where Slocum had almost gutted him. A week after that knife fight, they had been on patrol when a Yankee sniper had shot at them. Slocum had seen the bullet enter the side of Griggs's head. The man had fallen to the ground, kicking and moaning for Slocum to help.

Slocum had not bothered. Griggs might have been a comrade in arms, but Slocum had to restrain himself to keep from finishing the job the sniper had begun. He had ridden off, thinking the man would die in the dirt like a snake.

Slocum swallowed hard when he saw Griggs climb into the carriage beside the lovely Jessica. She drove. Griggs wasn't so much a snake waiting until sundown to die as he was a cat living the next of his nine lives.

"I'll make sure you're dead this time, you son of a bitch," Slocum said, "even if I have to cut your head off to be certain." Old hatreds died hard. That Braxton Griggs was somehow involved in Claudine's murder followed in Slocum's mind like day follows night. He owed Griggs from the war. He would torture the truth out of him to find out if he had anything to do with burning Devereau's shop—and killing Claudine. Killing Claudine always came to the top of Slocum's thoughts.

Slocum rounded the carriage house in time to see the tall twin doors closing. The three guards remained inside with the rifles. Jessica and Griggs drove off with a rattle and a clank. Slocum hesitated for only a moment. The rifles would stay put for some time. But where a lovely Southern belle from Brazil and a former guerrilla in Quantrill's Raiders were going together piqued his curiosity.

A few horses tethered nearby drew his attention. Slocum selected a sorrel that looked strong and ready to run, and mounted. The horse, protesting a new rider, tried to throw him. Slocum expertly controlled the horse, and turned its head in the direction taken by Jessica's carriage.

He trotted along until he caught sight of the carriage, then slowed to follow fifty yards behind. Jessica drove expertly through the narrow streets. More than one tough approached the carriage, only to fall back. Slocum guessed it was Griggs's presence that held the brigands at bay. They recognized sudden death in the man, in spite of the years since the war.

Slocum rode past each tough, and they let him go unmolested too. For that he was thankful. It would not do to have a ruckus draw unwanted attention. Slocum might be able to explain to Jessica why he was tracking her through the New Orleans streets, but once Griggs recognized him, the fat would be sizzling in the fire.

"Whoa," came the woman's sharp command. The horse drawing the carriage reared and tried to kick out. Jessica held the gelding in check, finally getting out of the carriage and dealing with the skittish horse herself. When the horse had calmed, Jessica tied the reins to a post and went around and spoke quietly to Griggs.

He took her arm as he climbed from the carriage. The pair of them went to an iron door mounted flush in a warehouse wall. Jessica rapped twice, then once, and gave the password.

"For the cause," Slocum mouthed along with her, though he could not quite hear her actual words. Both Jessica and Griggs entered. The door clanged shut behind them.

Dismounting, Slocum tied his horse to an iron rod protruding from a tumble-down building. He doubted the horse would be waiting for him when he came back. Too many thieves patrolled the waterfront for prime horseflesh like this.

Slocum patted his vest and the derringer stuck there. He wished he had brought his Colt, but going to a fancy-dress cotillion packing iron would have drawn too much attention to him. Not for the first time, Slocum longed for a shoulder rig and a small .32-caliber Smith & Wesson tucked into it.

"Might as well wish for a cannon," he grumbled to himself as he studied the ironclad door. Although he might bluff his way past a sentry on the other side of the door, Slocum knew that would only bring Braxton Griggs down on his head. Stealth had to win him what he wanted.

For now. When he got back Devereau's stolen merchandise, then he could concentrate on avenging Claudine.

Slocum walked along the warehouse until he found a drainpipe running down from the gutters lining the roof. Slocum jumped onto the pipe, tested the strength of the nails holding it to the wall, then carefully climbed until he reached the roof. Then he flopped over, getting his fancy duds dirty. He didn't care because he saw an open door leading into the warehouse—and Jessica.

He slipped into the dark heat boiling up from the guts of the warehouse. Going down a rickety ladder brought Slocum to the main floor of a room stacked head-high with boxes. He heard voices from near the door where Griggs and Jessica had entered, and thought those within the warehouse were greeting the newcomers. Slocum took the opportunity to grab a pry bar and hurry along the stacks, hunting for any hint of vault or safety box where Devereau's gems might be secreted.

One box in particular drew his attention, although it wasn't what he sought. Using the end of the bar, he levered off the lid and peered inside. It took him several seconds to understand what the multi-barreled device was.

"A Gatling gun," he said. Slocum poked through the excelsior, and found a dozen three-foot-long magazines for the weapon. He dropped the lid back and stared at the other boxes around him. After opening two more he realized he had blundered into a warehouse packed with munitions and ordnance. The paltry few crates of rifles stolen from the Federal Armory the other night added little to the firepower represented here.

He began counting. Forty crates of ammunition. Dozens of kegs of powder and dynamite. At the end of the stack he found two mountain howitzers like those used so effectively against the Apaches in Arizona. The short-barreled cannon could be swung around easily and fired fast, and delivered enough wallop to take out even a bank vault. When it was loaded with chain or grapeshot, a full company of infantry in front of that muzzle would be put at jeopardy.

"So Jessica's mysterious friend is serious about a filibuster," Slocum said. Bullock had never come out and said what the plan was. Vague claims of the South returning to its former glory weren't worth more than a cow chip in the hot sun—unless backed up by men and weapons.

How many men had signed on, Slocum couldn't say. But the weapons in this warehouse would outfit at least a company of men, maybe even a regiment.

The cocking sound of a six-shooter caused Slocum to swing around. He flung the pry bar as he turned, and this saved his life. The iron bar hit the guard in the face and caused the man's aim to go astray. But there Slocum's luck ended. The pistol discharged. The echo crashed back and forth through the huge room.

Slocum followed the pry bar with a hard punch to the man's face, driving him to the floor. Slocum kicked hard and grabbed for the fallen six-shooter. He lifted the six-gun and fired twice. The first bullet hit another guard rushing to see what had caused the disturbance. The man stopped, straightened, and looked down stupidly at the tiny red spot blossoming on his chest. He sank to the floor without making a sound.

Behind him came two more. Slocum fired again, hoping to drive them to cover.

Then the air filled with lead all around him. The two guards opened fire, and were quickly joined by three others who had climbed atop the stack of crates.

Slocum dived over the howitzer and rolled, coming up behind the stack of black powder kegs. A bullet drilled through the wood in front of his face, causing Slocum to jerk back. A thin trickle of powder fell out, giving Slocum an idea.

"I'll blow the whole damned place up if you don't back off," he called. Picking up a small keg, he tossed it as hard as he could. When it hit the floor, it cracked open and rolled a few more feet, leaving behind a gritty trail of black powder.

Slocum patted himself down, only to discover he had not brought any lucifers. That didn't matter to a man desperate enough to light the powder. He laid the six-shooter down near some of the spilled powder and fired it. The sparks spitting from cylinder and barrel ignited the powder.

It burned sluggishly toward the keg that had cracked open.

"Git outta here! The whole place's gonna blow!"

Slocum knew better, but took the confusion he had sown to hightail it along the warehouse wall. Before he reached safety, the crude black powder fuse fizzled out. None of the guards had ever worked with the powder, he guessed, and didn't understand how hard it was to keep the grainy powder burning. He would have been better off using a stick of dynamite from one of the cases—if he could have found a length of miner's black fuse and a blasting cap.

There was no time for any of that. He kept an eye peeled for any sign where the brigands might have hidden Devereau's stolen stones, but the warehouse seemed reserved for endless rows of crates, all filled with stolen military equipment.

Slocum dropped to a crouch when he heard feet shuffling against the floor in front of him, blocking the only way out Slocum knew other than the ladder leading back to the roof. Three men with rifles popped into view. Slocum lifted the six-shooter he had taken and fired. Only one slug sailed toward the trio.

They returned fire immediately, forcing Slocum to backtrack. He dropped the empty six-shooter and reached for the derringer tucked away in his vest pocket. He had two shots—against how many guards? Slocum had no idea.

"Over here, he's over here!" came the cry from behind. The would-be soldiers had gotten over their fear of the black powder and closed in on him. Being caught between three with rifles and an unknown number coming from the other direction presented a problem.

Slocum clambered up a pile of boxes, kicking and scrambling to stay low and get off the floor of the warehouse. He rose and found himself staring down the barrel of a rifle.

Two shots rang out simultaneously, one from the gunman with the rifle and the other from Slocum's derringer. The slug from the rifle went wide. Slocum's buried in the man's gut, doubling him over. As the rifle slid from a shock-numbed grip, the man grated out, "Here, he's up here!"

Slocum slugged him, and yanked the rifle free in time to get off three fast shots. None hit the men coming up onto the boxes after him, but it gave him a few seconds to run.

Jumping from one crate to another, occasionally firing the rifle to keep those pursuing him ducking and dodging, he reached the wood ladder he had used to get into the warehouse. Slocum abandoned the rifle and hurried up the ladder, ignoring the way it creaked under his weight and the splinters he drove into his tough palms.

Fancy clothes in tatters, bleeding from a half-dozen scrapes and cuts, Slocum tumbled onto the warehouse roof. He knew he had only a few seconds before the guards followed. Before they got the gumption to start climbing the ladder, he wanted to be far away. Slocum had accomplished nothing with this foray, and cursed himself for it.

What he had intended to find had slipped away. Even if Devereau's jewels were hidden here, they would be moved quickly once the leaders of the filibuster learned he had invaded their domain and gotten away.

Then even this evaporated.

"John, John, I had thought better of you," came a soft, lilting voice he recognized instantly. He turned to face Jessica. She held an under-and-over shotgun. Its muzzle never wavered from dead on target in the center of his chest. From the way Jessica smiled, he knew she would not hesitate to kill him.

"I had thought better of you, but then I always seem to discover the most capable of men." Her finger tightened on the trigger.

10

Slocum looked left and right, wondering how he was going to escape. If he dived over the edge of the roof, it was a long fall to the street—one he wasn't likely to survive. But that might be preferable to having a fist-sized hole blown through his belly by a load of buckshot.

Then Jessica relaxed. He saw it in the set of her shoulders and the way her trigger finger turned pink again, but he didn't see it in her face.

"You're different from the others," she said suddenly. "You followed me here. What is it you want?"

"Another waltz?" Slocum asked.

Jessica laughed. "You *are* a piece of work, Mr. Slocum. Come, let us go and discuss your future."

"If there is to be one?" Slocum asked.

"You have a good grasp of the situation. What I wonder about is your real interest in coming here tonight, other than my own charming self, of course." Jessica laughed even louder than before, but there was no humor in her voice. "I would hate to think you worked for the Federals. It would cause me ever so much pain knowing a man like you had thrown in your lot with scalawags."

Slocum made his way down the shaky ladder and dropped to the warehouse floor. He looked for an oppor-

tunity to hightail it, but Jessica was too careful. Any hint
that he would bolt and run would have spelled his demise.
By the time Jessica jumped down the ladder, a half dozen
of the guards circled Slocum. Their rifles were all dead
on target in the middle of his body. He didn't even consider running now. Better to bluff his way out since Jessica had hesitated killing him outright.

"The office," she said, flouncing off. The lovely bru-
nette did not even look back to see if the men obeyed.
From her tone she knew they would. Or else. Slocum eyed
the crates, and tried to estimate how many rifles and how
much ammo were cached there. It was enough to create
quite a fuss.

But not a war.

Jessica swung open a door and went into a small office.
Sitting at a desk in one corner was Braxton Griggs. The
grizzled old guerrilla stared right at Slocum, but Slocum
got a curious feeling. It was as if the man stared at him
but saw nothing.

"Sit down there, Mr. Slocum," Jessica said, pointing
her gun at a chair opposite Griggs.

"Slocum?" asked Griggs. "John Slocum?"

Slocum went cold inside.

"It's been a while since I saw you, Griggs."

"You left me for dead, damn you!"

Slocum shifted slightly in the chair, but Griggs did not
follow the movement. The dull appearance in his eyes told
Slocum Griggs wasn't likely to be engaging in gunplay.
He was blind.

"The sniper got me, too, Griggs," Slocum lied. "I got
laid up for months, then the war was over."

"Ah, you two know each other," Jessica said in an
appraising tone. "How interesting."

"We both rode with Quantrill," Slocum said.

"I've heard about Griggs's problems," she said. "A
bullet took him in the head and left him blind. But you,
Mr. Slocum, you surprise me. I would not have pegged

you as fitting in with Quantrill's Raiders. It is not often a man can continually give me pause, sir.''

"I'll take that as a compliment," Slocum said. He watched Jessica from the corner of his eye, but he stared at Braxton Griggs. Where the blind guerrilla fit in was beyond him.

"And I'll consider you a challenge," Jessica said. "Mr. Griggs is an advisor.''

"Advisor?" asked Slocum.

"The general," Griggs said cryptically. "The general asked for help in planning. I was always real good at that, even when I rode with Quantrill.''

"I remember," Slocum said. And he did. Quantrill and Bloody Bill Anderson would get together for night-long drunks to plan their raids, but more often than not it was Griggs's brutal strategy they employed to such violent effect. Griggs had been shot down before the Lawrence, Kansas, raid. Otherwise he would have been there brutally gunning down the boys under eight—and maybe even the girl children and their mothers. Any plan Griggs came up with never took into account loss of life.

Except when it was his own life.

"He done shot up four of us real bad," chimed in a guard standing in the doorway, fingering his rifle. "Shoot the son of a bitch, and let's get on with it.''

"He made fools of you," Jessica said sarcastically. "That's why you want to kill him.''

"Al's had one or two thoughts in his day," came another voice Slocum recognized instantly. "This might be a good one." Bullock pushed his way into the room. The bullet-headed man stood massive and ominous, glaring at Slocum. "I tried to recruit him. He was there when we got the rifles from the arsenal, but no one saw him after.''

"Thought I was killed, didn't you?" asked Slocum. "Ask Griggs how hard it is to kill me.''

"I'll do the damn job myself!" shouted Braxton Griggs. He stood, knocking over his chair and flailing about. "Gimme a knife! I'll cut his throat!"

"You tried and couldn't do it, Griggs," Slocum said coldly. "Blind, you don't have a snowball's chance in Hell."

"I'll do it for you, Griggs!" shouted Al. He cocked his rifle. Slocum got ready to get out of the way when lead started flying. In the small room the irate rifleman might wing Griggs or Bullock. But then Slocum saw the expression on Jessica's face. For all the bad blood between him and Griggs, she remained calm—and deadly.

The shotgun she held never wavered. Slocum would have his head blown off before he could move an inch.

"Gentlemen, calm yourselves. This is not a matter we should decide. It ought to be left up to the general," Jessica said.

"Why bother him? Slocum's a traitor," said Griggs.

"So I was supposed to walk into the mouth of a Yankee cannon and die?" Slocum shot back. "The others you recruited, Bullock, all of them died in that damnfool attack. Am I a traitor because I didn't get myself ventilated? I wanted to join the filibuster then, and I still do now. That's why I came here, to see how good you all were."

"He has a point," Jessica said. "You should not have used him in the shock troops, Bullock."

"He snuck in!" protested Griggs.

"I wanted to know what was going on," Slocum said. "That was the only way I was likely to find out. Bullock wasn't going to tell me, and after trying to kill me with a suicide mission, I wasn't overly inclined to ask him."

"There are many questions requiring answers," Jessica said. "How did you know to go to the party tonight? Why did you follow me?" She shook her head. "No sugary tall tales, John, please. I've heard them all."

"With you in the lead, I'd follow anywhere," Slocum said, half meaning it.

Jessica laughed. "You were wrong in how you dealt

with him, Bullock. And you, Griggs, you don't know it didn't happen the way he said.''

"He left me for dead," Griggs grumbled.

"I caught a bullet myself," Slocum said, "I was in no shape to rescue anyone, much less you. There was never any good feelings between us, Griggs. And I thought you *were* dead." That carried the ring of truth in it because Slocum meant it. After all these years, the last man he expected to see alive was Braxton Griggs.

"Let the general decide," Bullock said.

"Mr. Griggs, let's find him," said Jessica. "Al and the others can guard Mr. Slocum until we return."

"He'll want to see you floatin' facedown in the Mississippi," Griggs snarled. "You might be square, Slocum, but I can't forget what's gone on between us. The general will agree with me." Griggs made a stabbing motion with his hand.

"Come along now," Jessica said gently. She took the old soldier's arm and guided him from the room. With Jessica leading him, Griggs hardly appeared blind. He stepped easily, and slipped through the doorway without breaking stride. Slocum got the idea they had been doing this for some time. Braxton Griggs wasn't the kind to trust just anyone.

"I may have made a mistake, Slocum," said Bullock, "but I don't know. I seen what you done out in the warehouse. That makes you look like a spy to me, but I can't figure who you'd be reporting back to."

"I want some excitement in my life," Slocum said. "You asked me to join the filibuster, not the other way around."

"There's more to you than shows, Slocum. The general will know what to do. He knows everything." With that, Bullock followed Jessica and Griggs into the warehouse. The sound of their heels vanished as they left.

Al and another gunman blocked the door, their Winchesters leveled at him. Al obviously thought real hard about plugging Slocum, while his companion nervously shifted his weight from foot to foot. He didn't keep his rifle pointed in the right direction. Slocum didn't consider him too much of a threat. Yet.

Slocum settled down into the chair and hiked his feet to the desk. He leaned back to consider how long he was likely to live after Griggs spoke with the mysterious "general." Slocum thought this might be the man who had accompanied Jessica in the cemetery when O'Leary had been killed. He hadn't gotten a good look at the man then, but the general commanded a passel of men with modern ordnance and wielded more power than was good for any man not in the army.

And Slocum had no doubt that the man heading the filibuster lacked real military training. Why else depend on a man like Braxton Griggs for advice?

"You kilt my best friend," Al said. He fingered the rifle trigger to the point that Slocum hoped it hadn't been worn down to a hair release. An accident now meant a bullet through his head.

"He tried to kill me first," Slocum said, not caring which of the men in the warehouse Al had counted as his friend. "What does it matter? This is war, right?"

"It will be when we we're ready to take over," Al said.

Slocum slid his heels around on the desk, finding some papers. With a sudden movement that appeared accidental, Slocum's boots slid out, sending him off the chair and to the floor. He hit hard and lay there, unmoving.

"The stupid son of a bitch knocked hisself out!" Al said with a laugh. "He slipped, and the chair went out from under him." Al and his companion laughed.

"What are we gonna do, Al?" asked the other guard.

"Let's go kick his ribs in," Al said. Slocum heard the steps approaching. He pictured it all in his mind, then reacted when both guards were in range. A hand closed around the leg of the chair he had tipped over. The chair swinging into Al's knees brought forth a yelp of pain and a rain of rifle, and chawin' tobacco, and the man's hat as he flailed about.

Slocum got his feet against the wall and shoved hard. He rocketed out and tackled the other guard. They both went down in a heap. Surprise gave Slocum an instant's advantage. He took it. His fist mashed the man's face. Spinning around, Slocum scooped up the guard's fallen rifle and aimed it at Al before the other man recovered.

"You—" That was all Al got out before Slocum swung the rifle butt around and smashed it into the man's jaw. The sick crunch of wood breaking bone was quickly drowned out by Al's moans of pain. In spite of the agony he had to be feeling from the broken jawbone, Al went for his six-shooter. He fumbled and wrapped his fingers around the butt of a Colt shoved into his belt. A second wallop on the top of Al's skull put him out cold.

Slocum panted harshly, then sat on the edge of the desk to catch his breath. A quick look into the warehouse assured him he hadn't attracted any attention from whoever might be out there—if anyone was. The way Jessica had spoken suggested to Slocum that she and Griggs and the others were all abandoning the warehouse to go fetch their mysterious general. He searched the downed men and took their six-shooters. Sticking them into his belt made him feel more dressed.

He looked down and laughed at that. His fancy duds were filthy and in tatters. But he still sported all of Devereau's diamonds at his cuffs and the large headlight stickpin. Somehow this, with his stolen six-guns, made him feel as if he could whip the world.

The thought of Devereau and his stolen gems caused Slocum to take a few minutes to search the desk and the lone file cabinet in the corner of the room. All he found were old shipping orders for cotton and hides. The warehouse office had not been used in some time for anything more than a meeting place for the filibusterers.

"They surely wouldn't be filing paperwork on a warehouse full of stolen rifles and cannon," Slocum said to himself. He checked Al and the other guard. Both were still out cold. Slocum considered taking the time to tie them up—or just put a slug in each of them. He owed them no mercy. They thought they were leading the charge to establish a new Confederacy. Slocum considered how much better off they might be dead.

He left them. There wasn't any reason for him to waste good lead.

He stepped into the warehouse, wondering which way Jessica and Griggs had gone. The deep shadows and lack of light made it hard for him to determine where he was and how best to get out of the warehouse. One route out he knew for certain was to retrace his way up the ladder and get onto the roof. From there he could get to the street level—and walk off. Slocum didn't fool himself about the horse he had stolen still being tethered where he had left it.

"Or I might just get lucky and find where Al left his horse. He didn't look to be the kind who enjoyed walking anywhere." Slocum found a warehouse wall and started following it. Halfway around the far wall he found a doorway. Picturing the layout in his mind, Slocum reckoned this was the doorway Jessica and Griggs had used to get into the warehouse earlier when he had followed them.

He might find another door. He might find Al's horse. He might grow wings and fly off too. Slocum tested the door and found it unlocked. He opened it slowly, peering out into the street. It surprised him that it was almost daylight outside. He had been in the warehouse a lot longer than he had thought.

Stepping out, Slocum took a deep breath of the fresh air. He caught the wetness and fish smell of the Mississippi, but also the hint of freedom on the breeze.

The sound of a hammer cocking froze him.

"You make life so interesting, John," said Jessica,

moving around from behind him with her shotgun leveled.
"Griggs bet you wouldn't get away."

"How much did you win?"

Jessica's laugh told the story. Simply being right was
enough for her.

11

Slocum waited to die. But Jessica's finger never tightened enough to set off the shotgun. A smile danced on her bow-shaped lips. Then she grinned and dropped the muzzle of the weapon so it pointed at the ground in front of Slocum.

"I don't know what to make of you, John. I want to believe. I do. You are so capable . . . in so many ways."

"They were going to kill me," he said, jerking his thumb over his shoulder in the direction of the warehouse office where he had slugged Al and the other guard.

"You'd say that, of course, no matter what happened in there. I have no doubt Al wanted to make life miserable for you, however, and got exactly what he deserved. He is not too intelligent a man." She came closer and ran her fingers slowly up and down his tattered coat lapels. "All I'd like is to make life lovely for you." She kissed him quickly and stepped away. "But can I trust you? I simply cannot come to any conclusion on that."

"You waited for me to escape," Slocum said, half accusing. If Jessica was unsure what to make of him, he was even more confused about her motives.

"I did," she said. "Griggs went on back to get some sleep."

Slocum glanced up and saw the sun rising. He shrugged

this off. When a blind man slept mattered little, he supposed. Sleeping during the heat of the day might not be such a bad idea.

"I had to find out how good you really were, and I don't mean with a six-shooter. Escaping so easily, so quickly, shows how truly formidable you can be. Even Bullock says you are capable, and it is hard to impress him."

"I told Bullock I wanted to join up."

"But why?" Jessica said, frowning in mock concentration. Slocum reckoned she had already thought about this at some length. "You are not a patriot, even if you were an officer in the CSA. What happened is not something I want to explore, but you seemed to have ended your military career on a sour note."

"Getting shot in the belly did change my mind about a lot of things," Slocum said.

"See?" she said. "There it is again. A touch of truth that hides the real meaning. How can you tell the truth and yet deflect my questions? You are a most fascinating man, John. And because of that, I am willing to test your loyalty to the New South once more."

"No more being put in a suicide squad?"

Jessica laughed a siren's laugh, and Slocum was willing to believe anything she said. She took his arm and steered him from the warehouse to her carriage.

"Organizing a filibuster requires a certain willingness to die, John, but to answer your objection to the other night's mission, tonight will be dangerous but not intentionally so. We had to get those rifles in a hurry, and expending a few raw recruits was viewed as an acceptable price to pay."

"Why kill a dozen men for a few crates of rifles when you have a warehouse full of ordnance?" Slocum asked.

"You do go on with those questions, don't you, John? Come along now. Bullock is already forming the company for this evening's raid. You must prepare."

"Right away?" he asked. He sat on the carriage seat, his thigh pressing warmly into Jessica's.

"Afterward, John, after you have displayed your bravery and dedication to the cause." She pointedly moved away from him.

"For the cause," he said automatically. She eyed him a moment, her varicolored eyes twinkling. Then Jessica snapped the reins and got the carriage moving quickly along the New Orleans streets. Slocum wondered what he was getting himself into.

Slocum hunkered down, holding an empty Spencer rifle. The tubular magazines for the weapon were stacked in front of Bullock. Bullock walked back and forth slowly in front of the two dozen men. As before, Slocum considered those alongside him to be nothing more than cannon fodder. That Bullock did not trust them with ammunition—yet—told him more about the raid than anything Bullock passed on from the general.

Slocum heard many of the men talking about "the general" in hushed, awestruck tones, but no one had ever seen him. He was a military genius. He had won battles and even wars in Latin American countries. He was the only real patriot left, and had to be the one to unchain the South from the yoke of Reconstruction and lead them all to newfound freedom.

For all the respect the recruits showed for the leader, none had seen him.

During the day, Slocum had not even caught sight of Jessica again. He wondered if she would be taking part in tonight's raid, as she had in the one on the Federal armory.

"Slocum, you lead the first squad," Bullock said, snapping Slocum's attention back to the situation at hand. "What do you do?"

"Chop down a couple trees, drag them across the railroad tracks, and then douse it all with kerosene," he said.

"Good. You wait until you hear the train whistle. It always whistles as it rounds Deadman's Bend. You set fire to the logs so's the engineer has plenty of time to stop."

"That's when the other squad attacks," Slocum said. "We lay down covering fire, if there are Federals on guard in the back of the train."

"Exactly. Murphy, you take your men and blow open the mail car. We might as well see if there's anything' worth stealin'. The rest of us will go for the flatcars and the howitzers there."

Slocum drifted again as he listened to Bullock quiz Murphy and his men about unloading the cannon and moving them through the swamps. What Bullock eased past was the chance the shipment was protected by more than a handful of soldiers. After the raid on the arsenal, the Union forces would be more alert—and maybe out in force to keep cannon and shot from falling into the wrong hands.

The general was assembling quite an arsenal, but Slocum hadn't seen the men required to use it, if the filibuster was to succeed. Going up against the entire army of the United States with a handful of zealots was an even more futile endeavor than the Southern states seceding and then standing together.

"Smitty! Get the wagons!" Bullock shouted. To his platoon, Bullock said, "Captain Fontaine has scouted the area. He'll meet us there with any last-minute instructions. To the wagons! For the cause!"

"For the cause!" echoed the recruits. Slocum joined the cry because he was aware of Bullock staring at him. From what he could tell, Bullock reported directly to Jessica—or maybe Braxton Griggs. Griggs had eyes among the troops, of that Slocum was certain. Whatever else he thought of the blind guerrilla, Slocum knew Griggs was not a stupid man.

He would know everything going on in the filibuster

or he wouldn't have any part of it—unless the gain out-weighed the risk. At this, Slocum struggled to figure out what Griggs got out of the filibuster. Money? Stealing rifles from an armory hinted that money was in short sup-ply. That the filibuster might succeed was so remote a possibility that Slocum would sooner bet the sun would rise in the west the next morning.

"Git yer ass in, soldier," snapped the wagon driver. Slocum jumped in and dropped to the rough bed in time to keep from being thrown out as the driver gee-hawed and got the team pulling.

"When are we getting the ammunition?" he called out to Bullock, sitting beside Smitty in the driver's box.

"When the time is right," Bullock said. "Now shut yer tater trap. We're goin' in quiet-like."

The rattle and clank of the wagon and the puffing of the horses made that goal unattainable. Slocum figured Bullock didn't want to talk with any of his underlings. Sitting back, Slocum stared out into the darkness. Here and there he saw the winking of a lightning bug hunting for a mate. Hungry sounds from deeper in swampy terrain told Slocum getting off the road wasn't a smart thing to do.

He looked his fellow filibusterers over, and decided it wasn't worth striking up an acquaintance with any of them. They all looked too determined to be heroes. Not a one was over twenty. He couldn't deny them their en-thusiasm or misplaced patriotism because he had seen it too many times before—and had even felt a tad of it him-self when he had joined up. A good officer could make a man *want* to die for a cause, no matter how crack-brained.

All the men riding along the mosquito-infested road with him were fired up and ready. Slocum saw a repeat of the prior debacle at the armory. One squad was sacri-ficed as a diversion while the other did the thieving. It was a good tactic as long as you didn't mind losing the men providing the diversion.

The general obviously considered this a worthy battle plan.

"Bullock! You are late!" came the reprimand from the shadow of a banyan tree. Riding out from under a low-hanging limb came the white-haired Colonel Demeter. Beside him walked Fontaine, wearing a plain butternut Confederate officer's jacket. The piping and insignia had been removed, but the captain's insignia remained on the collar tabs.

"We're ready for the mission, sir!" barked Bullock, jumping to the spongy ground.

"Excellent. Captain Fontaine will lead your squads into position. I will take up my station. We have less than fifteen minutes to prepare! Do your duty, sir!"

"For the cause!" answered Bullock.

Demeter rode away into the darkness, leaving Fontaine and Bullock huddled together, gesturing and arguing over what to do.

"Slocum, Murphy, assemble your squads!" yelled Bullock, turning back to Fontaine.

Slocum motioned and got his ragged men in a line. Murphy let his mill about like dogs without a master. Slocum knew this fight was going to end in disaster unless better discipline was maintained. Like the discipline of the three men who had killed O'Leary in the cemetery.

"Move 'em out," came the order. Slocum held back. "What's wrong, Slocum? Not clear enough an order for you?"

"The magazines. I want my men to have ammo before we head out. Two tubes each, four if you've got them."

Bullock and Fontaine exchanged looks. Fontaine looked disgusted, then headed off through the undergrowth. His boots made squishy sounds as he walked, but they soon vanished in the natural noises welling up from the swamp.

"We're late," Bullock said. The bullet-headed no-necked man planted himself in front of Slocum as if he wanted to have it out. That would have been fine with Slocum.

"What kind of firefight can we mount without bullets?" Slocum asked. "You want us to drop our rifles and throw rocks?" From behind he heard his men begin to whisper among themselves. They had been all het up to attack, and had forgotten their rifles were empty.

"Yeah, he's right," piped up a young man who looked barely sixteen. "I can shoot the eye out of a squirrel at thirty yards. I ain't gonna shoot myself or anything I ain't aimin' at!"

"Me too," chimed in another. And so it went until Bullock saw full-scale rebellion on his hands if he didn't give in.

"Get the ammo. It's in the wagon," Bullock said. He glared at Slocum.

Slocum didn't ask the obvious question of how they were supposed to use cartridges left behind when the shooting started. He thought he knew the answer. Smitty and his wagon would drive on to where the real soldiers would be resupplied.

"Take four each," Slocum ordered. "Put one magazine in the butt of your rifle and stuff the other three into your belts where you can get to 'em when you need 'em."

Bullock swung about and stormed off. Murphy's squad trotted behind, letting Slocum and his men bring up the rear. It took about ten minutes to reach the tracks. Several axes had been dropped beside the railroad tracks.

"Git your men sawin' down trees, Slocum," ordered Bullock. "There's a gallon of kerosene to douse the trunks. You got a way of settin' fire to it when you get the signal?"

Slocum patted his shirt pocket. He had a tin of lucifers. He nodded.

"Murphy, get yer squad moving. You come with me. We'll be under Colonel Demeter's direct command." Bullock glared hotly at Slocum, his eyes buried in pits of gristle as he squinted. "You better not mess this up, Slocum. You do and you'll answer personally to the general!"

"I'll do my duty," Slocum said.

Bullock grunted and headed off with Murphy and his men trailing behind like drunken ducklings following their mama.

When Bullock was out of earshot, Slocum said to his squad, "Don't worry about sawing down trees. Get broken limbs, anything that's already fallen and dried out a mite."

"Good idea, Slocum," said one of the young men. "I was a-wonderin' how we'd e'er get green wood to burn."

"Rocks," Slocum said. "Get big rocks and put them behind the wood on the tracks." This sparked a laugh from the young man who'd just spoken.

"You ain't from aroun' heah, are ya, Slocum? This is *swamp* land, not mountain. We'd stand a bettah chance of rollin' a gator onto the tracks."

"Get two gators," Slocum said, grinning. "We want to be sure the train really stops!"

The men set to work with a humor that had been lacking before. Barely had they gotten the tracks littered with wood and doused it with the kerosene than a mournful whistle cut through the swamp.

"The train's at Deadman's Bend," Slocum said to his men. He reached into his pocket and pulled out a lucifer. He struck it and tossed it onto the firewood, although he had not received Bullock's signal to do so. He stepped back as the flames shot ten feet into the air.

Slocum didn't care if the fire burned up the sparse wood. All he wanted was a big enough wall of flame to make the engineer throw on the train brakes.

A gunshot seconds after the wood ignited gave Slocum the official orders.

"Check your rifles. Get a round in the chamber," Slocum ordered. "And don't go shooting at anything that

moves. You'll fire when I give the order and not before—
or I'll cut your ears off and feed them to the nearest gator!''

This produced another round of chuckles from the Louisiana boys. Slocum took them onto the far side of the
track, opposite where he thought Bullock would have
Murphy's squad stationed. As they strung out along the
track bed, the freight train hove into view. The engineer
had applied the brakes, sending foot-long orange sparks
dancing off the rails into the night.

''Hold your fire, hold it, hold it, now!'' Slocum
shouted.

Three or four of his men might have fired. This was
about all he expected. In real combat most never fired
their rifles, being too scared or too caught up in the moment to even hear the command.

From the first volley Slocum knew they were in for a
world of trouble. Dozens of bluecoated soldiers jumped
from the cars immediately behind the engine. Bullock—
and the mysterious general—had pitted two squads
against an entire battalion. Slocum's squad mostly turned
and ran into the swamps when they saw the overwhelming
force facing them.

A few remained with him, and Slocum felt a respon-
sibility for getting them out in one piece. If that was possible, if Bullock and Demeter had ever intended for them
to do more than distract the main force of the Union soldiers.

''There, that way,'' Slocum ordered, pointing down the
tracks toward the caboose. A dozen freight cars and several flatcars along the way showed the ordnance the general intended to capture. But one by one, Slocum's squad
was picked off by the soldiers' withering fire. Slocum
reached the first flatcar and jumped onto it, the magazines
thrust into his belt clanking against the wood as he rolled
over and over.

He used the metal-clad butt of his rifle to knock down

a Federal sergeant, then swung his Spencer around and
fired several times. He hit one soldier and sent others running for cover. Grabbing the edge of a cover, Slocum
yanked. Four mountain howitzers were secured to the flatcar by strong rope.

"Bullock!" he shouted. "Fontaine! Here!"

From out of the darkness came the two men. For a
moment Slocum felt as if he had returned to the days of
the war. The butternut uniform looked the world like his
brother Robert's. But Robert was dead, killed in Pickett's
Charge.

"Cut the ropes and you got four cannon," Slocum said.
He flopped onto his belly and emptied his magazine in
the direction of an approaching squad of soldiers. Whatever remained of his squad was now dead or captured.
Slocum yanked out the empty metal tube and cast it aside,
slamming in another and emptying it lickety-split. A third
magazine slammed in, but the officer commanding the
Federals had a sudden attack of prudence, and held his
men back until he could see what they were up against.

Knives flashed in the dim moonlight, and the four cannon were pushed off the flatcar onto the ground.

"Damnation, this one busted a wheel!" came Bullock's
complaint.

"Leave it. Take the other three," ordered Demeter.
"Hitch those mules up now, Smitty. Move, man, do it,
do it *now*!"

From the adjoining freight car Slocum heard scraping
sounds and men grunting. He fell back and saw what remained of Murphy's squad struggling to move powder
and shot from the car. They dumped it directly onto the
bed of Smitty's wagon, though the driver was hitching up
mules to the howitzers.

"Get out of here!" Slocum ordered. He ducked as the
air filled with flying lead. The officer leading the Federals
had finally decided a frontal assault would win the day.
In Slocum's mind, the only thing worse than the officer

making a decision was him making the right one. Slocum jumped to the ground, vaulted over the howitzer with the broken wheel, and took off in the direction where the other cannon had been dragged.

Limbs caught at his face and tore his clothing. Twice Slocum slowed, turned, and fired into the night to keep the pursuit at bay. And for more than an hour Slocum was lost in the swamp intent on sucking his feet into gooey mire.

Eventually he found tracks left by the cannon and the wagon laden with the shot and powder for them. Slocum swatted at biting bugs and gritted his teeth, and suddenly came into a clearing lit by the wan moon. Standing in the center of the field were the three cannon, looking as if they had been dipped in silver. Beside them Smitty grumbled as he worked to load all the stolen shot and powder into caissons.

A straight-backed man mounted on a large black stallion supervised the operation.

Slocum didn't have to be told he had just found the general.

12

"Spy! Shoot him!" came the cry from the direction of the men gathered around the stolen howitzers.

Slocum stood for a moment, wondering what to do. He was exposed and had nowhere to run. The swampy land he had crossed was twenty yards behind him, too far to reach before a slug found his back. Seeing the futility in running or fighting, he did the only thing open to him.

"It's me, Slocum!" he yelled, holding his rifle high above his head and walking forward. "I got those howitzers for you!"

"Hold your fire!" barked the man on horseback. Controlling his shying stallion, the rider cantered toward Slocum. A long black cloak fluttered on the humid night air. Moonlight caught the man's face and turned parts to shadow, others to silver. Slocum thought he ought to be able to recognize him, but could not.

"You were the soldier who defended so well while we retreated?" he asked.

"Don't remember seeing you in the fray," Slocum said. Past the horse Slocum saw Bullock and Fontaine. As always, the two argued. Then Bullock came stomping over to stand beside the rider.

"Sir, this is John Slocum. He was in charge of the squad what stopped the train."

"A masterful fire that was, sir. And you successfully held off an entire regiment."

"Been meaning to ask one of you about that," Slocum said. "Where'd they come from and why weren't there enough men in my command to do anything about them?"

"In and out, strike fast, fade into the swamp," the rider said.

"It was another damned suicide mission, if you ask me," Slocum declared.

"Then it's good no one ast you yer damn opinion, Slocum!" Bullock shouted.

"A moment," the rider said. His stallion tried crow-hopping, but he held the high-spirited animal in check. "I ordered the attack. Are you criticizing my plan?"

"Yours, Demeter's, whoever thought it up," Slocum said. "You sent my squad in to die. I know that has to happen, but a good commander usually tells his men what's expected of them."

"Oh, the men knew their duty," the man said.

"Like hell."

"Slocum!" bellowed Bullock. "This is the *general* you're talkin' to!"

"Then I've come to the right place to lodge my protest," Slocum said. He saw no reason to back down now. He had bluffed his way this far. If he faltered, he would end up as dead as all the boys he had led against the train and its load of Federal soldiers.

"It's all right, Bullock," said the general. He dismounted and came over to Slocum. His cape swung away from his body, swirling like a black mist as he moved. Slocum felt the breeze from the yards of cloth as it came to rest when the general stopped.

Slocum looked the man square in the eyes. Although tan and well built, the general had an air of frailty about him. And Slocum noticed the same lilt in the man's voice as he'd heard in Jessica's.

"You from Brazil?" Slocum said, taking a shot at the man's background.

"I hail from the *sertão* outside Sao Lourenço. Are you familiar with this fine Southern colony?"

Slocum shook his head. "I don't rightly know what a *sertão* even is."

The general laughed heartily. "A man of honesty. So refreshing! I am Frank McMullan, Commanding General of the Army of the New Southern Confederacy." He thrust out his hand. Slocum shook it. Again, on the surface, McMullan was hale and hearty, but Slocum felt a twinge of weakness that made him wonder about this self-styled general.

"I don't rightly know what we're doing here either," Slocum said.

McMullan looked thoughtful. He put his arm around Slocum's shoulders and steered him toward the three how-itzers.

"You have given us a great start, Mr. Slocum, aiding us so well this evening."

"I joined up because of Bullock's recruiting, but all I've seen so far is a pair of missions where I was sent in to get killed."

"But you escaped alive and are well, Slocum," McMullan pointed out. "That makes you the type of man I need for my army. For you see, I have returned after leading a colony of Southern refugees for many years."

"In Sao Lourenço," Slocum guessed.

"Yes, yes, you are so perceptive."

Slocum wondered if praise like this endeared Mc-Mullan to those who followed his banner. It only put Slo-cum on guard. Nobody spooned out such honeyed words without wanting a bucket of blood in return.

"You see, Mr. Slocum, we fled when it became obvi-ous the Confederacy was on its last legs. Jeff Davis was a fine man, but not the one to have led us to victory over the Yankees. The Southern colony was well received by native Brazilians, and we have flourished there.

"Of course, there are problems with not living in the land of our birth." The man coughed and quickly covered it with a brush of his hand over his mouth. "Damn weather," he murmured. "It has become time to return and take what is ours by birth!"

"The South? Your filibuster is to seize the entire South?"

"Mr. Slocum, you *are* perceptive. But I hear the doubt in your voice. A sane man knows it is impossible. I assure you I am sane, but I intend to succeed, a little at a time."

"We'll take New Orleans first," said Bullock, who had trailed them like a puppy dog following its master. "The people will rise up and join us once this is a free city-state."

"Yes," McMullan went on, his eyes gleaming in the dark as his passion mounted. "The rebellion will spread like wildfire after I have shown the one true path!"

"For the cause!" cried Bullock.

"For the cause," Slocum said more slowly.

"I am uniquely qualified to lead the New South," McMullan added. "I learned my trade as a filibusterer under the famous William Walker."

Slocum thought about pointing out that Walker was executed when his filibuster to Nicaragua went awry. Everything Slocum had heard of the man told him he was a terrible leader and crazy as a bedbug.

"There is a fine tradition of filibuster lurking just under the genteel surface of New Orleans society," McMullan went on. "The Baratarians, of course, but we are their successors! We even meet in some of the old centers of rebellion."

"Maspero's Exchange," Bullock said. "And Banks' Arcade." Bullock stared at Slocum, as if challenging him.

The Magazine Street rendezvous spot was familiar to

Slocum from the first mustering after Bullock recruited him. They had left there for the Federal armory and nothing but a wagon load of death.

"A rebellion—a filibuster—needs men as much as it needs rifles," Slocum said. "I saw the warehouse."

"Ah, yes, Jessica mentioned your contretemps there. A sorry situation, for which I apologize. A man of your obvious military acumen ought not be inconvenienced in such a fashion." McMullan pulled Slocum closer and then released him, spinning around theatrically. His cape flowed out, then dipped back, barely brushing the ground. "You have proven your skill in battle, sir. I am hereby promoting you to the rank of captain!"

"But General McMullan," protested Bullock. "You don't know—"

"I am a good judge of character. Mr. Slocum—*Captain* Slocum—will make a fine addition to our command structure, Major."

"Major?" Slocum raised an eyebrow and tried to keep from laughing. Major Bullock?

"Sir, if you say so, then—"

"I *order* it, Major Bullock," McMullan said imperiously. "Now, we have to get our newly liberated ordnance to safety."

"The warehouse?" asked Slocum, fishing for information.

"Hardly, Captain. We will take it to . . . another location." McMullan was turning cagey now that Slocum was pressing him for details. As long as he could talk grandly in sweeping generalizations, McMullan wallowed in the words like a hog in slop. But Slocum felt the undercurrent of fraud in everything McMullan did and said, including his commanding presence. If he didn't know better, Slocum would have thought Jessica was the power behind the general.

"You ride in the wagon with Smitty," ordered Bullock.

"We got to get out of here pronto. I don't know how long 'fore them Yankees will git on our trail."

"Not long," said Slocum. He saw no reason not to tell Bullock of his encounter with the soldiers. "I discouraged them a mite, but they seemed determined to follow."

Slocum grabbed for the side of the box when Smitty cracked the reins and got the team moving. The heavy load of powder and three-pound cannonballs in the rear shifted. Wood creaked, but no one took any notice of it. Slocum decided not to either. Still, it made him uneasy with so much explosive rattling around just a couple feet behind him.

"You ridden with the general long?" Slocum asked.

"Naw, I joined up after him and the others come up from Sao Lourenço a couple months back," said Smitty. "But I heard 'em talkin' and knew where my destiny lay. Not been right with them carpetbaggers pourin' down out of the North and stealin' us po' folks blind."

This reminded Slocum of Braxton Griggs. "Did Griggs come up from Brazil with McMullan?" He didn't ask about Jessica, yet he knew she had lived in South America a spell too from the way she spoke. Both her speech and McMullan's carried a curious lilt that wasn't Spanish but definitely owed itself to another language. Slocum recollected that the people in Brazil spoke Portuguese.

Smitty grunted something Slocum didn't understand. Slocum rephrased his question.

"Who all came up with General McMullan?" Slocum asked. "Seems like he'd have a cadre of officers to build on."

"Some of the finest," Smitty said, as if coming to the conclusion he could talk freely to Slocum. "And some you'd never in a thous'nd years guess on."

"Like the woman with the mismatched eyes?"

"Miss Jessica?" Smitty laughed harshly. "She's one of his best tacticians, thass for sure. Mostly, he came with the idea and is buildin' up his legion of liberation now."

"For the cause," Slocum said sarcastically. Smitty missed the tone entirely and rambled on.

"We got the munitions, and we got the men. Now all we need's the word from the general and we'll all be on Easy Street, runnin' New Orleans like it ought."

"There was a powerful lot of Yankee soldiers on that train. Did you know about them before the raid?"

"No, but it don't surprise me much," Smitty said. He reached into his shirt pocket, took out a plug of tobacco, and bit off a chaw. He munched a couple times, spat, then held out the plug for Slocum. He shook his head. Second-hand chewing tobacco wasn't his poison.

For hours they rode, until Slocum began to nod off. Smitty hummed to himself, and kept the team pulling until they staggered from exhaustion. When the wagon creaked to a halt, Slocum came fully awake and looked around. They had reached a spot so desolate Slocum wondered if even Smitty could find their way out of it.

"Purty place, ain't it?" the man said. "This is the only dry land in the whole danged swamp."

Slocum saw a few tents pitched to one side of the marshy area. Men stirred and came out, some reaching for rifles stacked in pyramids outside their tents. Others were too sleepy. This was Frank McMullan's army.

Pounding hooves caused Slocum to turn and look behind. Up rode Colonel Demeter. The man had a flushed expression and looked wild-eyed and ready to fly off the handle.

"Get to training these men, Captain," he shouted to Slocum. "The general wants them turned into marksmen and artillery specialists by nightfall."

"Why me?" asked Slocum. He blinked some of the sleep from his eyes. He had not slept well on the rocking, bumping wagon, and pushed back exhaustion.

"The general said you were a first-rate officer, that you rode with Quantrill. You know how to drill and how to train marksmen. Snap to it, Captain!"

Slocum shrugged. Then he thought hard. Demeter had to have talked to someone other than McMullan to know his military history. Or had McMullan discussed him with Bullock—or Braxton Griggs? Demeter spoke in clipped tones, but Slocum thought he might have the same Brazilian lilt to his words that both McMullan and Jessica showed.

"I'll swing one of them field pieces round for you to practice with, Slocum," said Smitty. The wagon driver jumped to the ground and began unloading cannonballs and powder.

Slocum rubbed his stubbled chin and felt his belly growl. He was tired and hungry and wanted nothing more than to be a hundred miles from this camp. McMullan had no chance at all of winning over New Orleans. Even if a miracle occurred and the citizens of the city rushed to support the filibuster, it would take only a few days—a week at the most—for the Federal troops to surround the city and cut off river travel.

No Mississippi River traffic, no food. The railroad passing through town would serve as a pipeline funneling troops *into* New Orleans. Reaching the city by land was treacherous, with large lakes and alligator-filled swamps protecting it—and isolating it, at the same time. New Orleans had surrendered fast in 1862, the first major Southern city to fall to Union attack. It was vulnerable then, it was vulnerable now. For all the filibustering history written in blood along New Orleans streets, most of the illegal expeditions had been directed south out of the country, not inward.

"Set up a target in yonder grove," Slocum ordered one gangly youth.

"What do I use?" came the slow, drawled question.

"Your head, if you can't find anything else," snapped Slocum. He was no training officer. He lacked patience. And after two hours of firing the cannon and having one crew after another fail to do more than scare birds in the

swamp beyond the target, Slocum switched to rifle in-
struction. In spite of most of the men's more than passing
acquaintance with rifles and shotguns, they never quite got
the idea of firing in unison, with a purpose, and coordinated with others in their squad.

"Quite a crew, isn't it, Captain Slocum?" asked Demeter, reining in his horse just a few feet from where
Slocum stood behind a line of prone would-be marksmen.
"They are fine examples of Southern heroes. Don't you
agree?"

Slocum looked up at the popinjay of an officer and
answered, "Colonel, I've never seen men use rifles like
they do." The colonel missed the sarcasm woven throughout Slocum's response.

"Excellent, excellent. I shall report your success to the
general!" With that, the ersatz colonel rode off into the
swamp to tender his account of Slocum's capable training
techniques.

Foolish officers, blind tacticians, undisciplined soldiers,
bad marksmen, and stolen ordnance. One improbability
after another piled up in the filibuster camp. Coupled with
the United States' testiness about the possibility of New
Orleans ever seceding again, McMullan's filibuster
seemed destined for failure.

If the man intended to capture New Orleans.

13

"Captain Slocum!" called Frank McMullan. The filibusterer rode up on his magnificent horse. The stallion reared, McMullan jerked at the reins, then dismounted, handing the horse over to a young boy who had joined up just that morning. McMullan brushed the dust from his natty uniform laden with medals and enough gold braid to fence in the entire swamp.

"What can I do for you?" Slocum shouted. He wiped sweat from his face. The recruits had slowly gotten the idea of how to load and fire a howitzer, but the ring in his ears from round after round fired, both with and without shot, had nearly driven him crazy.

"Good practice," McMullan said, looking at the willow Slocum and his artillery crew had blown to splinters. Slocum didn't tell the man it had taken eight rounds to reduce the tree when, at this range, it should have been done in one.

"They're learning," Slocum said. His sooty-faced crew smiled at this. He had not been too lavish with his praise during their training.

"Set up a target about the size of the side of a barn," McMullan ordered. Three of the recruits trotted off to construct it.

"Ought to be able to hit *that*," Slocum said under his breath. "Or maybe not."

"We need to move one of the cannon into New Orleans this evening," McMullan said. "We will strike at midnight."

"Strike what? The armory? The soldiers will be waiting for us. Once stung like they were, they'll be real attentive to anything moving along the road outside the arsenal."

"We have enough rifles, Captain," McMullan said loftily. "We need funds to pursue our goals."

"Funds? You thinking on using the cannon to blow open a bank vault?" Slocum scratched his head. He had never considered such a thing. More than one bank had fallen to his six-shooter over the years, but never had he considered stealing a cannon and turning it against the steel doors of a vault. "You're going to have to be careful not to blow everything in the vault to hell and gone."

"The cannon will get us into the bank. Using it against the vault itself is not possible since, as you pointed out, it would destroy the contents we seek."

"So we blow down the door with the cannon? We could use a battering ram, if making noise isn't a problem."

"There is more, Captain, there is more to my plan. You shall see." With that McMullan spun about, letting his cape theatrically billow and sink back around his ankles. He pointed like the captain of a ship sighting land for the first time. "Your target. Hit it, sir!"

"Sight in!" Slocum bellowed. His crew jumped to the task. They swabbed the hot metal barrel to cool it. They rammed in both charge and three-pound cannonball, and set the firing pin. Then, on Slocum's command, one swung a hammer down. Hammer struck pin and the mountain howitzer belched smoke and ball.

For the first time all day, they had lined up perfectly. The cannonball sailed smack dab in the center of the target.

"Excellent, excellent," cried McMullan. A hint of insanity shone in his eyes. "New Orleans will be mine! The new South will lead the world!"

"For the cause," Slocum murmured, then went to congratulate his crew. Then they cleaned the cannon and loaded it into Smitty's wagon for the long journey into New Orleans.

"When, Captain, when do we set up our gun?" asked the green recruit. He had not learned the lesson most veterans learned, of napping until battle. He paced and grumbled so much Slocum considered using him as the cannon ram.

"When we get our orders," Slocum said. He stared down the deserted street. Music and loud cries of drunken frivolity drifted over from the French Quarter some half a mile away. The Bank of the South on St. Charles was quiet, having closed more than five hours earlier. Traffic along this section of the road proved sporadic. All in all, robbing this bank made sense to Slocum. The way McMullan intended to do it was wrong, though. Too much noise before the vault yielded its treasure would bring the New Orleans police on the double.

What was McMullan really up to? For all the flashes of sheer insanity, he had equal flashes of genius. The self-styled general played some game other than filibuster. Of that Slocum was certain. While it took a pile of money to finance a filibuster, McMullan might have already accumulated it through theft of Devereau's emeralds, the diamonds from his burned-out shop, and the loot of who knows what other robberies.

Slocum gritted his teeth when he remembered his last minutes with Claudine. There hadn't been any reason to kill her, or try to kill him by burning down the jewelry store around his ears. The thief had already taken the gemstones and had gotten away with the crime. The fire and Claudine's death were unnecessary.

"Cap'n," came a low voice from one of Slocum's sentries. "We got company comin'."

Slocum rested his hand on the rifle he had been given. It had taken a lot of complaining, but Colonel Demeter had relented and given Slocum and his men rifles with enough ammo to hold off a small army. Demeter had at first insisted all Slocum needed was the cannon.

"Howdy, Colonel," Slocum called. The colonel jumped in surprise. He had not expected Slocum and his command to be so well hidden.

"Captain," Demeter answered. "The time is ripe for attack. Swing your field piece around and blow the hell out of the door!"

"I can get into the bank without causing such a ruckus. I scouted it and—"

"You had no right! You weren't told to do that!"

"I wanted to see how much powder I'd have to use," Slocum lied. He had been curious about the strength of a door requiring a cannon to blow it down. It was sturdy, but not anything that wouldn't fall to a pair of men with a battering ram. He could be through the door and into the bank to blow the vault in seconds. The drama of cannonade wasn't necessary. Not for this bank robbery.

"Then use the proper amount. Fire when you get the range!" Colonel Demeter stormed off. Slocum heard the man's horse whinny and then hoofbeats going away—fast.

"Listen up," Slocum called to his crew. "One shot, then we get the hell out of here. Understand?" He frowned, knowing how hard it would be to clear out if anything went wrong. Smitty had brought them by wagon and left quickly after they had unloaded the howitzer. There had not been any arrangement for them to rendezvous after completing the mission.

Slocum considered how best to correct this oversight on McMullan's part.

"Three of you, go steal us some horses. Enough for us

to ride and an extra to hitch the cannon carriage to.''

"Steal 'em? Shore, why not, Cap'n?'' said one burly red-haired youth hardly old enough to shave. "I done that before I jinned up, and not far from here either.''

"Get to it. The rest of you, at ease until they get back.''

"Uh, Captain, what's going on? Don't we go on in and bust open the vault? The general wanted what's inside, didn't he?''

"We weren't ordered to do that,'' Slocum said, this striking him as even stranger. Why blow the door down, then not give orders to clean out the vault? No one had even mentioned this, not McMullan, not Bullock, and not Demeter. Slocum admitted to himself that nothing about the filibuster was professional. For all McMullan's self-praise, he was no commander. And he was not much of a robber either.

"Why not? Some other unit goin' in?''

"Reckon so,'' Slocum said, eyeing the way the cannon was set up and pointed down the street. The range was less than fifty yards: point-blank for a mountain howitzer. There wouldn't be kindling left of the door when they hit it. And that bothered Slocum even more. Bullock and Demeter had sent him on two prior suicide missions. This one carried the foul stench of another assignment intended to kill off the men carrying it out.

After ten checks on the cannon elevation, the chocks under the wheels, and every other detail, Slocum heard the men returning.

"Got 'em, Cap'n. A couple swaybacked nags, but one for you that's right purty. A sunfishin' bronco, but you're a good rider and can handle him.''

"Crew, prepare for firing,'' ordered Slocum, wanting this to be over and done.

"We're ready, Cap'n,'' said the slight sandy-haired youth holding the firing mallet.

"Get our horses ready,'' Slocum ordered the red-haired

horse thief. "We will abandon the howitzer, if it comes to that."

"What are you sayin'? There's no reason to get all yellow-bellied and run," protested the boy. "We stole that popgun fair and square. The general won't like it none if we leave it behind."

"Do it," snapped Slocum. "Horses ready for all of us."

He checked the alignment of the field piece one last time. He clapped his hands over his ears, turned away from the cannon, and shouted the order. A second later the howitzer belched out its load of cannonball and smoke. The hot iron ball whistled through the air and crashed dead on target. The explosion when the ball hit knocked Slocum and two others off their feet.

"Glory be," shouted the sandy-haired recruit who had fired the cannon. "We did that?"

"No," Slocum said, shaking his head to clear it. Whatever had happened was independent of the cannonball. There had been the initial impact and then a short delay before the ground had shook and orange flame erupted from the shattered bank windows. Even if they had intended to rush in and loot the vault, that chance was gone now. The bank blazed merrily, setting fire to adjoining buildings. In the distance clanged a firebell.

"Hitch up the howitzer," Slocum ordered. "Leave the caisson. It'll only slow us down. We got to get out of here—" He cut off his command to withdraw when he saw the street filling with blue-uniformed policemen.

"Coppers!" shouted one of Slocum's men. "Wait, no, them's soldiers. Yankee soldiers!"

Like an inexorable tide, the line of infantry marched down the street away from the bank and directly toward Slocum's position. They came fast, and they had bayonets fixed. The troops had to have been ready for any disturbance to get into position for attack this fast.

"Load the cannon! Tamp the powder, get to it!" Slocum shouted. The crew had been trained well enough to obey.

"What about swabbing it down? We'll melt the barrel if—"

"Melt the damned barrel," Slocum snapped. The Union troops had cut the distance in half, and now their sergeant ordered them into a full run. Slocum saw the youth was having trouble getting the ramrod out. Slocum pushed him out of the way, grabbed the mallet, and smashed it down on the firing pin.

The cannon roared, belching out cannonball and ramrod. Slocum wasn't sure if the rod didn't do more damage than the ball. The soldiers parted in disarray, not expecting this violent an attack. Slocum motioned his crew to the horses.

"Get out of here! Ride like your lives depend on it!" Slocum realized how close to the truth this came. They had been sent into the jaws of yet another trap. Only coincidence and the brief training of his artillery crew had saved them.

"Captain, the way's blocked," came the unnerving report from the first of the crew to mount and start away. "Looks to be New Orleans policemen for real this time."

Slocum stood in the stirrups and stared past the men ahead of him. The report was accurate. A dozen New Orleans policemen had drawn their pistols and were trying to assemble into an organized assault. Slocum levered a round into his Spencer and put his heels to his horse's flanks. With a rebel yell, Slocum charged through the middle of the policemen.

He didn't stop to see if his men followed. He fired wildly, not caring if he hit any of the police. All that mattered was scattering them and letting him get past. Behind him, the Federal sergeant had reformed the disorganized troopers and had them firing. The ragged volley took one of Slocum's men out of the saddle, hitting in the middle of his back. And then Slocum rushed past the police.

"They's shootin' their own men," called the sandy-haired youth. He stayed low on his horse's neck and raced along beside Slocum.

A quick glance behind showed Slocum the truth of the observation. The soldiers were firing through the rank of New Orleans police, who shouted in anger and returned fire using their pistols. What had been a clever flanking movement had turned into disaster for the soldiers and police.

"Let 'em kill each other. We done it, Captain! We did it!"

Slocum had no idea what it was they had actually accomplished. The shell had ripped open the bank and then the rapidly spreading fire—after the secondary explosion— had guaranteed no one would be able to loot the bank vault. If Demeter or Bullock had men inside the bank, even seconds after the shell knocked down the door, they had died.

But Slocum hadn't seen another squad moving to take advantage of the breached door. Nothing of this operation made any sense, including McMullan's continued conniving to get his men killed.

What worried him most of all was the speedy appearance of both U.S. Army troopers and a platoon of New Orleans policemen, all armed and ready for a big fight.

It was almost as if they had been expecting the bank to be robbed by McMullan.

"Split up, lose yourselves in the French Quarter," Slocum ordered. "Get on back to the camp by sundown tomorrow. Don't get caught, don't let any Federal spy trail you," he finished. The men gave him sloppy salutes and rode away, intent on finding some barrel house or bagnio to while away the hours.

Slocum turned his horse in a different direction. In

twenty minutes he reached Pierre Devereau's humble house.

"Mr. Slocum, I had thought you were gone. I would not have blamed you." Devereau sniffed. The small Frenchman wrinkled his nose and wiped at it. "You reek of gunpowder. What have you been doing these past days?"

"Trying not to get killed," Slocum said, not wanting to elaborate. He pushed past Devereau and went into the sitting room. He dropped wearily into a chair and took off his hat. He wiped black soot from his face and tried not to get it onto the neat, clean armrest.

"You look terrible," Devereau said. "I trust there has been some progress toward finding Claudine's killer."

"Not too much," Slocum admitted, "but I'm on the trail of your diamonds and emeralds."

"So little. Gladly would I trade them all for my dear Claudine's killer."

"I think I know who did it," Slocum said.

"Who? You have found—?" Devereau bit off words, making Slocum sit straighter in the chair. It had sounded as if Devereau had almost named his daughter's killer.

"You know who did it?" Slocum's words snapped like a whip.

"I saw only a glimpse," Devereau said.

"How'd that happen? You said you were here in the house asleep. Why didn't you tell me you caught a glimpse of Claudine's killer?" Slocum was outraged at the jeweler. Everyone was working hard to keep him in the dark. McMullan and Demeter and Jessica were playing a hand he did not understand, and now he had discovered by an accidental slip of the tongue that Pierre Devereau was hiding information from him too.

Of the two groups, he was madder at Devereau. Slocum wanted to find Claudine's killer as much as her father.

"I heard horses in the street that night," Devereau said. "I went to look and saw a dark figure moving toward my shop. I dressed and . . .'' He choked up. He swiped at tears welling in his eyes. ''I should not have taken so much time. I got across the street quickly in time to see the thief riding off and . . . the fire and Claudine was dead and you were injured. Oh, how could I have been so slow! To have been faster would have saved my precious Claudine!''

''Was the robber about my height?'' Slocum asked. He went on to describe McMullan the best he could.

''I . . . I cannot identify him so well from your description, but if I ever see the killer again, I will know it.''

Slocum felt he was missing something important, but short of beating it out of Devereau, he wasn't sure how he could find out what it was. Let the man hide information from him. Slocum was sure McMullan had committed the crimes of theft and murder before covering them up with arson.

Slocum leaned back in the chair and studied Devereau carefully. The man would accept the return of his stolen gemstones, but he wanted revenge. That didn't bother Slocum too much. *He* wanted revenge too. But first he had to be sure McMullan was the one on whom to heap his vengeance.

Plans began churning in Slocum's brain. It was time to stir the pot and see what bobbed to the surface.

14

Slocum peered into the carriage house behind the house in the Garden District. He was not too surprised to find that the wagon loaded with the rifles stolen from the Federal armory had been moved. McMullan might have ordered it out to the bivouac in the middle of the swamp, or he might have cached the arms in the warehouse down by the levee. Wherever they had been taken, Slocum wasn't too inclined to hunt for them.

He was more interested in the guests arriving at the fashionable house. Moving like a ghost, he went up onto the back porch. Two Negro maids bustled about in the kitchen preparing silver trays of food. From around the side of the house came low voices in intimate conversation.

Slocum ducked around and took a quick look. Two men standing at the side of the spoke in guarded tones. From the cut of their clothing, both were wealthy beyond Slocum's dreams. One puffed furiously on a big cigar. The other gestured grandly. Snippets of his words reached Slocum.

". . . if he finds out? McMullan looks to be a vicious man if crossed."

The one smoking the cigar shook his head disdainfully.

"He is a fool. Look how he parades around like some damned peacock. It's the woman I would worry about. She might just be the true leader of the whole affair."

"We double-crossed them. So what?" The harsh laugh told Slocum the two thought they had duped ignorant bumpkins. He wasn't certain he wanted to be in the men's shoes—but then he thought McMullan had killed Claudine. He would parade the filibusterer in front of Devereau for a positive identification, then put a bullet in the man's head. It was more than McMullan deserved. But first he had to pry the man loose from Demeter, Bullock—and Braxton Griggs.

"When will we get the money from the insurance?"

The cigar-smoking man shrugged. "Does it matter? We'll both be so rich after the settlement, we can afford to wait a few weeks."

"Weeks! I have gambling debts!"

"Carson, shut that mouth of yours or I'll do it for you," the man said. He puffed on the cigar, got an ash glowing, then stubbed it out against the side of the house. "Let's get on back inside and enjoy some of the general's fine champagne."

Carson frowned, obviously troubled by his own double-crossing and the lack of an immediate reward. Slocum didn't know what the two had done, but they might have been bankers.

Bankers who insured their defunct bank for thousands of dollars after looting the vault. A filibusterer had come along to blow open the bank. Then they had torched it and arranged for both the New Orleans police and the U.S. Army to be there to nab the thieves.

From the way they spoke, McMullan didn't know about the double-dealing. They had probably told him the police—or even the soldiers—had stolen the loot from the vault.

The telltale click of a hammer being cocked froze Slocum in his tracks. He glanced up to the second-floor balcony. Jessica stood there with a derringer pointed in his direction.

"I do declare, John. You turn up in the oddest places at the oddest times."

"Evening, Miss Jessica," he said, touching the brim of his hat in a polite acknowledgment that she had the drop on him. A derringer at this range wasn't much good. Even if she were the best shot in Brazil, he could dodge and get away. Slocum didn't want to escape. There were too many unanswered questions. And the gems to retrieve for Devereau. And Claudine's death to avenge.

He wasn't sure which of those reasons drove him the hardest. Looking up at Jessica as she sighted along the short barrel of the derringer, her mismatched green and blue eyes coolly appraising him, Slocum wasn't sure she didn't figure prominently in his reluctance to simply ride away.

"I ought to plug you, John, I really should. You abandoned your post under fire. That's treason."

"To the New South?" he asked.

"What else? For the cause, John. You did not live up to my high expectations for your bravery."

"That might be because it was a trap set by the bankers," he said, taking a guess at all he had overheard.

She eased down the hammer of the derringer, then tucked it into the low bodice of her dress. Jessica licked her bow-shaped lips, then gestured to him.

"Do come up, John. Let's discuss this matter further."

He caught the drainpipe at the corner of the house and shinnied up until he was even with the balcony where she stood. Digging his toe into the metal strap holing the pipe to the house, he kicked out and jumped, his fingers curling around the balcony railing. He swung over and landed lightly beside her. Inhaling deeply, he caught the scent of her jasmine perfume.

"What did you mean?" she asked.

"I overheard two men saying how they'd duped the

general,'' Slocum said. ''Can't rightly recognize them since they were in shadow below us, but it sounded as if they were bankers.''

''How could they have possibly double-crossed us?'' she asked, more curious than angry.

''Clean out the vault, put a few cases of dynamite in the lobby, then wait for the cannonball to come crashing through the door. When was the vault supposed to be cleaned out?''

''What? Why, after—'' Jessica bit off her words. She now realized what Slocum was talking about. ''The building was supposed to burn down and our soldiers, disguised as firemen, were to cart off five hundred pounds of gold under the noses of the police.''

''The explosion took away that chance, didn't it?''

''It did go up more than anyone had guessed.''

''Except the bankers. And they stand to get insurance money for the loss too. Might be they owned all the buildings around. Why'd they ever agree to be part of this robbery?''

''Bankruptcy afflicts banks too. Carson and Malone had driven their bank into shallow financial waters and were going aground. They were to share in the proceeds and blame the bank failure on the robbery.''

''Duped,'' Slocum said positively. He didn't move away as Jessica came closer to him. Her perfume excited him. And then he found so much more to do that job.

Her fingers stroked over his face, then worked behind the back of his head before pulling his face down to hers. She kissed him. Hard. Their lips crushed together; then hers parted slightly. Her darting pink tongue invaded his mouth and explored. He worked his own tongue over hers, and soon they were engaged in an oral hide-and-seek, their tongues fleeing and hiding and caressing until their passions became unstoppable.

''Inside, John. We can't, not out here where anyone can see.''

"Why not?" he said, enjoying the shocked expression on her face. For once he held the upper hand. He stroked over her lustrous hair and down her back until his hands rested on the sleek curves of the pert behind hidden under layers of billowing dress.

He pulled her tightly against him and kissed her again.

Jessica pushed back slightly and said in a husky voice, "I wish it didn't take so long to get out of these skirts. They can be such a bother at times."

"Not too much of a problem," Slocum said, working at the lacing on her bodice. Eyelet by eyelet was freed until her warm, lush white breasts spilled out. Jessica grabbed and caught the derringer she had stuffed in there. She smiled wickedly, her finger on the trigger. Then she tossed it over her shoulder onto the balcony floor.

"I won't be needing that kind of gun," she said. "Not when I can find something *so* much better." Her fingers slid down Slocum's chest and burrowed between his belt and his belly.

He sucked in his breath when her questing fingers found the pillar of manhood growing a bit lower. She stroked awkwardly over it, then withdrew her hand to work frantically at his pants.

"There!" she said in triumph as his long, hard shaft jumped out. Slocum gasped as she lightly kissed the tip. Then Jessica started stroking along its length, and teased the hairy sac dangling beneath until he was unable to stand any more.

"Enough of that," he said. "I want to get you out of those skirts."

"That'd take too long," Jessica said, panting with heightened passion. "Here, here, John, do it this way!"

She dropped to the floor, then rolled onto her hands and knees. She pulled up her skirts until her bare white bottom appeared. Slocum stared down at her, a curious sense of reliving this moment hitting him hard. At first he couldn't figure out what was going on. Then he remembered how he and Claudine had spent her last minutes in the jewelry shop.

"What's wrong? Getting second thoughts?"

"No," he said, dropping behind her. He ran his hands over the sleek snowy curves of her rump. Then he circled her waist and pulled her against his body. They both groaned in pleasure when his length slid forward and parted her nether lips. Jessica jammed her hips backward and took him deep into her most intimate passage.

The lovely woman excited Slocum—and at the same time filled him with a sense of foreboding. This was so much like his last moments with Claudine, yet it wasn't. Jessica and Claudine were nothing alike.

"Don't wait, John, don't, don't. Move!" Jessica rotated her hips, stirring him around inside her. This was more than enough to push Slocum in the direction they both desired most.

He began thrusting, slowly at first and then with more power and passion. Gripping her around the waist, he held her in place so she didn't scoot away accidentally. Then he reached forward and brushed over her dangling breasts. The light touch of his hand across the tips of her pendulous breasts made her gasp and throw back her head as if she was a bronco trying to buck him off.

But she wasn't trying to get rid of him. All around his length came incredible, erotic pressure as her excitement soared uncontrollably. She moaned and sobbed and rocked through her climax. Slocum kept up the easy hip movement, in and out, until her heat and pressure on him caused him to lose control.

He pistoned harder and faster until the carnal heat along his shaft lit explosives deep in his body. Erupting, he pumped furiously until entirely spent. He was aware of Jessica climaxing again, but it was as if someone had clipped his senses free of his body. He knew what he was doing—and another part of him insisted on coldly comparing what he was doing now with the last assignation with Claudine.

"Oh, John, don't ever stop surprising me," Jessica said. She rocked forward, then lay on the floor, staring up at him. Her mismatched eyes were so enticing, so exotic. She shivered lightly, and it caused her breasts to shiver. Her nipples were still rigid and bright red and her face was flushed from the climax.

"You're the mysterious one," Slocum said. "If I live to be a hundred years old, I'll never figure you out."

"A lady likes to be . . . mysterious. That is such a good description," Jessica said in a low, sultry voice. "Would you like to be mysterious with me again?" She reached out, but Slocum backed off.

"Pleasure and business shouldn't mix too much," he said.

"Not *too* much, but they ought to be mixed. That adds spice to the experience." Then Jessica scowled a little. "What business are you talking about?"

"The bank robbery didn't get the money you need for the filibuster, did it?"

"No," she said tartly. "If what you say is true, it might be difficult to ever get the money from those scalawag bankers."

"They only used the soldiers for their own purpose. I doubt their sympathies lie with north."

"If you ain't with us, you is ag'in us," she said in a mocking tone. "They cheated the general. That means they are our enemies."

"Might be. I figure they are out to line their own nests," Slocum said. "That doesn't make them your enemies."

"If they're not our allies, they are our enemies," Jessica said, a hint of steel coming into her words. Slocum knew it was now or never if he wanted to get to the heart of revenge.

"You don't have the money from the bank you need," Slocum said. "I can help you."

"Steal it from Malone and Carson?" Jessica snorted, then reached down and began lacing her bodice, as if signaling it was time to get down to business and to forget pleasure.

"They're too clever for that. It would take more time to unearth the money—the gold," Slocum said. He watched as Jessica straightened her skirts and stood, picking up the derringer she had thrown down. She tucked it away safely between her breasts, reminding Slocum how dangerous this Southern belle was.

"Bullock is an accomplished man when it comes to torture," she said with malice. "They crossed us."

"I can sell the diamonds and emeralds for a good price," Slocum said, taking his best shot. For a moment, he thought Jessica was going to draw the derringer and use it on him. A wild storm of emotion crossed her face, her green and blue eye taking on a crazed look. Then she settled down.

"What do you know about such things?"

"I ran into one of the Live Oak Boys who stole a package of emeralds. This made me curious. I heard about a jewelry store robbery a little later. Both crimes seemed pointless since there was no way any of the gang could sell what they stole—unless they were hired by someone who knew what they wanted and how to get it." Slocum didn't bother relating how he had seen her and McMullan in the cemetery before the policeman was killed after trying to extort the gems from them.

"You are too curious about some things, John. I *do* wonder about you. Who are you working for?"

"My own best interest," Slocum said easily. "I used to gamble on the riverboats until I got tired of it."

"And they stopped being so lucrative. Everyone travels by train these days," Jessica said.

"I made quite a few friends along the Mississippi,"

Slocum went on. "A passel of diamonds might be hard to sell in New Orleans. But not farther north."

"How much farther north?" Jessica said. "We don't have much time."

Slocum wanted to ask what the pressing deadline was, but refrained. He had made her suspicious of his intentions already. Too many questions would spook Jessica.

"Not far at all. My, uh, friend is traveling this way soon. He has a hefty line of credit with several local banks."

"We'd need gold," Jessica said.

"To back the New South scrip?" Slocum asked. He saw Jessica was going to lie by the way her eyes blinked rapidly, even if she did stare directly at him when she answered.

"Of course. What else? How much do you think you can get from your friend for the stones?"

"Can't rightly say until I can tell him how many and what quality we're talking about."

"That seems fair," Jessica said. Slocum held his breath as the woman went inside to the far side of her bedroom and reached behind a wardrobe. She fished around for a few seconds, then drew out a small blue velvet bag. Slocum held his breath, thinking he had hit the jackpot. Then Jessica upended the bag and poured out three small, shining diamonds into the palm of her hand. From all Devereau had told him, this was only a small fraction of the stones taken from his shop. And none of the emeralds was in the bag.

"Take these stones," Jessica said. "I can get more, many, many more. It will take a day or two to fetch them, since they are stashed elsewhere, but I am sure the, uh, general will authorize it if you get decent value for these."

"And the emeralds?" Slocum asked. "My friend has a special interest in them. He says they are harder to come by than diamonds."

"That is true," Jessica said in an offhand manner, as

if she was dickering for a better price. "DeBeers controls the supply of diamonds, and currently there is such a glut on the market to keep prices—and their control—in line with their desires. But emeralds?" She shrugged her shapely shoulders. "They lie beyond the control of the international gem dealers."

Slocum took the diamonds and closed them in his hand. So close, so very close. And still he had no way of recovering all the stones. Or being sure McMullan was responsible for Claudine's death.

Yet.

15

"We need to know how much money you can get soon, John," Jessica said.

"When?"

Jessica smiled crookedly and shook her head, as if chastising a small child for mischief. "You know I can't tell you a thing like that."

"Why not? I'm a captain, aren't I?"

"Even Colonel Demeter is not privy to such information. Only the top advisers know."

"You and Braxton Griggs?" Slocum asked.

The storm cloud coming over Jessica's tanned face promised an angry outburst, but she held her tongue. She took a deep breath to calm herself. Slocum watched her carefully, wondering how such a lovely woman could have thrown in with such evil men.

"Find what you can get for the stones. I'll get the rest, if your price is adequate."

"Very well," Slocum said, tucking the diamonds into his pocket. He considered kissing her before he left, then decided against it. She might rip his face off. The anger he had brought to her by asking about Griggs seemed out of line with her usual equanimity. Something about Braxton Griggs and Jessica stayed concealed from him.

151

"The way you came in," she said suddenly. "Go out that way." Jessica pointed toward the balcony. Slocum shrugged. He didn't mind jumping over the balcony as he had done before. It seemed curious to him that Jessica wasn't willing to let it be known to anyone else in the house that he was in her boudoir. Jessica had not seemed overly concerned with her reputation before, so this meant she was hiding their assignation from Frank McMullan.

Or Braxton Griggs.

Slocum looked down onto the grassy lawn, then vaulted the balcony and landed heavily. He glanced over his shoulder, thinking Jessica might be watching. She wasn't. That told Slocum all he needed to know. He hurried away, knowing she was sending one of McMullan's underlings to track him.

Slocum had not reached the front gate by the time he heard footsteps behind him. He didn't bother looking back. Whoever Jessica had put on his trail was a terrible tracker, hardly bothering to conceal his presence. As Slocum walked along briskly, he considered this. Maybe the one blundering along behind him was meant to make Slocum overconfident. Another, better tracker might also be after him. Jessica had a lot riding on Slocum getting a fence to buy the diamonds.

Even in a sophisticated town like New Orleans, it wasn't easy getting rid of precious stones at a price that would make stealing them worthwhile. Slocum guessed McMullan had stolen the gems as a way of getting portable wealth, but now that the bank robbery had cut off his flow of greenbacks, McMullan needed the money to press on with his filibuster.

Slocum walked briskly to Canal Street and then down toward the Mississippi, cutting over into the Vieux Carré until he found an alley. A quick change of direction, a sprint, and an open door afforded Slocum the chance to lose the man on his trail. Slocum waited a few minutes, then peered out the door. A second man hurried along.

When he stepped into the light of a gas lamp Slocum saw the man's face.

Bullock. He had forgotten about him. Somehow it did not surprise him much that Jessica trusted Bullock with such a mission. Bullock looked around, grunted, and stalked off hunting for Slocum.

Backtracking, Slocum left the French Quarter and headed for Pierre Devereau's home. He knocked twice before the jeweler answered.

"Mr. Slocum," he said, rubbing sleep from his eyes. "Do you not ever sleep?"

"Things are jumping," Slocum said. He pulled out the diamonds and held them out for Devereau's inspection. The jeweler took them in a shaky hand and held up one. He said nothing, but went to a cabinet, pulled out a jeweler's loupe, and shoved it into his eye.

"One of mine. You have recovered my stones?" Slocum saw the expectation—and the rage—on the Frenchman's face. If he had not guessed it before, he knew it for a fact now. Pierre Devereau wanted to kill McMullan himself as revenge for Claudine's death.

Slocum felt a pang of guilt, but it passed. That was going to be *his* province, not Devereau's. McMullan would pay for killing Claudine—with one of Slocum's bullets in his foul heart.

"These are all," Slocum said. "They were given me because I promised to find a fence. The filibuster needs money, and they're willing to sell off their booty."

"Can you get the rest? And the emeralds?"

"I think so. What would these be worth?"

"A thousand dollars," Devereau said.

"I'll offer five hundred then," Slocum said. "That ought to set well since they will know that no one buying them would pay anywhere near full price."

"May I keep these?" asked Devereau. His hand curled around the stones and squeezed so tightly Slocum thought blood might flow. "Claudine wanted this one set into a pendant. I never had the time to do it for her."

"I'll get back as soon as I can." Slocum hesitated, then asked, "You *can* identify the man who killed Claudine?"

In a level tone Devereau said, "I will know immediately when next I see the murderer!"

Something didn't set well with Slocum, but he had no time to delve into it deeply. Devereau was hiding something. But so was Jessica. So was McMullan. Everyone lied to him as fast as they tried to get him killed.

He struck out to return to the American District, but slowed when he saw that a crowd had gathered. This was New Orleans. To get a crowd as noisy and large required something out of the ordinary. Slocum stood on tiptoe trying to see what the police were doing. He turned and asked the scruffy man beside him what had happened.

"Don't rightly know," the man said. "Heard tell they found themselves a pair of fancy dudes all cut up."

"So?"

"So they wasn't robbed. Nobody took their shoes or coats. Course there was a lot of blood."

Curious, Slocum pushed through the crowd until he could look over the shoulder of a blue-jacketed policeman bending down. The cop shook his head sadly.

"Poor son of a bitch never had 'ary a chance."

"Neither did this one, Sarge," said another policeman. "He took a shiv in the back, then the killer worked him over good."

Slocum swallowed hard. The man on the ground with his throat slit from ear to ear was all too familiar to him. Banker Malone had paid for double-crossing Frank McMullan. He couldn't see the other corpse, but guessed it to be Carson. The two bankers would never spend the money they had stolen from McMullan. If he hadn't fully realized it before, it came home hard to him now. The filibuster was serious business and men ended up dead.

Like Malone, Carson, Texas Jack—and Claudine.

Slocum headed for the house where he and Jessica had

parted only a couple of hours earlier. Things were moving fast, almost too fast for him. But Slocum wanted to put an end to this and get the evidence he needed that McMullan was responsible for Claudine's death. How he was going to kidnap the man and get him to Devereau so the jeweler could identify him as his daughter's killer was hazy in Slocum's mind. But it revolved around fencing the stolen gems. McMullan needed money, and Slocum could provide it. That seemed a good enough way to set up McMullan for the bullet Slocum would put through him.

Slocum considered going to Jessica's front door and introducing himself, then remembered he had climbed her balcony before. No reason not to do it again. Slocum scampered up the drainpipe and made the jump. It was easier now that he knew where to grip and how to put his feet. Silently swarming over the balcony railing, he went to the partly opened French doors leading to her boudoir.

Slocum froze when he recognized the voices.

"He's trouble, Jessica. I don't buy his story about being wounded, not one damn bit," said Braxton Griggs angrily. "The son of a bitch left me for dead because he hated me, not 'cuz he was savin' his own worthless hide."

"He's got a mighty big scar on his belly," Jessica said. "That might be the proof he was gutshot like he claims."

"No tellin' how he came by it. Not legitimately, that's for sure," said Griggs.

"Better go now. He's supposed to be back soon with money for the diamonds."

"He'll turn on you, mark my words."

"He did lose the men I set on his trail," Jessica said, amused. "I figured he would. He's good, really good."

"He's a son-of-a-bitch snake in the grass," snarled Griggs. "You don't know what you're dealin' with in John Slocum."

"I think I do," Jessica said in an almost dreamy voice.

Then, with more bite in her tone: "Get on out of here now."

Slocum sat and waited fifteen minutes before making a big fuss that drew the woman's attention. Jessica opened the doors wide and saw him crouched on the balcony, as if he had just jumped up.

"You do have a problem with knocking on the front door." She grinned. "I like that."

"Then I've got some good news for you. My fence can give you a good price for the diamonds. Five hundred dollars."

"That's not as much as I'd hoped, but—" Jessica bit her lower lip, thinking hard. "I'll get the other stones. Give me the money, and we'll make arrangements for the rest."

"I can pick up the money in the morning," Slocum said. "You're not upset I left the stones with the fence? I think he has to go to someone else to get paid."

He'd expected fire and lightning over this. She surprised him with a negligent wave of the hand. "I trust you, John. After all, you came back when you might have ridden out of New Orleans."

"The men you set to following me weren't too good. I hope you weren't too hard on them."

"We have other matters to deal with." She glanced around, as if hunting for a clock. "The attack is soon."

"Attack? Another robbery?"

She shook her head. "Not now. The time for such money-raising is past. We now move to give power to the New South. Tonight we liberate New Orleans!"

Slocum was taken aback. He had failed to pick up any hint that McMullan would strike tonight—and strike where?

Jessica seemed to read his mind. "Come with me, my dear Captain Slocum. We'll check on the main body of troops. You can ride as my personal bodyguard." She didn't wait for an answer as she spun and flounced back

into her bedroom. Slocum followed more slowly, then
stopped in the doorway. Jessica was stripping off her
fancy dress and putting on a dark riding outfit. The sight
of her bare flesh appearing, then being hidden reminded
him of their lovemaking, but now she was all business.

All death. She strapped on a wide leather belt with twin
holsters. Thrusting six-shooters into the holsters, she settled the weight around her hips, then took a rifle from her
wardrobe. Inside was an arsenal rather than the yards of
clothing Slocum had expected.

"Here, catch," Jessica said, tossing him the rifle. He
caught it easily, checked the magazine, and found it fully
loaded. She took a second rifle from the rack and headed
for the door. Turning, she said, "Well?"

"I'm on my way," Slocum assured her. Downstairs the
few filibusterers in residence were already dressed and
armed to the teeth. Several of them looked like the guer-
rillas who had ridden with Quantrill, a half-dozen pistols
crammed into their belts to give incredible firepower. Slocum himself had ridden with ten pistols in holsters, stuck
in his belt, and carried in his saddlebags. He could rip off
sixty shots before having to reload. Not a single Federal
soldier had been able to withstand that kind of firepower.

Outside, a dozen horses pawed nervously at the soft
ground. Slocum took the nearest one, and no one seemed
to mind. Beside Jessica, he rode fast through the sultry
night, until his horse began to lather up from the frantic
pace.

"We're killing our horses," Slocum said. "If we need
to ride anymore when we get to the battle, we'd better
rest them."

Slocum saw that two of the men agreed with him. Bullock was openly hostile, maybe because Slocum had lost
him so quickly earlier in the evening. Of Braxton Griggs
there was no trace. If the blind man was going into the
fight, it was by some other route.

"Battle?" she scoffed. "There is no *battle*. There will be *battles*."

"You have enough men for that?"

"Of course we do. The general is no fool. He knows surprise is important and can be used in the place of a large army, but there is no substitute for soldiers. We will double our effectiveness tonight."

"There's the railroad tracks," Bullock shouted, standing in his stirrups and pointing.

"And there is our force," Jessica said so softly only Slocum heard. He saw dim shapes moving about, ripping out a rail and letting it roll down a cinder-packed slope into a bog.

"This is only one line into New Orleans," Slocum said. "There must be a dozen more."

"Eight others, and all are being destroyed." Jessica's words were cut off by the high-pitched screech of a train whistle. Slocum saw more men moving into position, training a howitzer on the bend in the tracks where a train had to slow.

"Troops," Jessica said. "They will be blown to bloody pulp by our cannon. There are more than a hundred snipers out there in the trees, also. This will show the Yankees they cannot move their soldiers into New Orleans to reinforce their garrisons."

Slocum saw that this would force the Federal commander to bring in his soldiers on horseback and by foot along any of the roads meandering through the swamps.

"There's the Mississippi," Slocum said. "A single riverboat can bring in more troopers than you can possibly fight off."

"To the levee," Jessica ordered. "You think we're fools, John. We have plotted this ever so carefully. We know the way the Yankees think and where their troops are stationed."

Slocum rode alongside the woman, deep in thought. Behind them came the throaty roar of cannonade, followed swiftly by the sharp snap of Spencer rifles firing from ambush. The railroads moved men and matériel quickly. Jessica was right that the Federals would be crippled with the tracks pulled up and their troop trains ambushed.

But how could McMullan and his filibuster hope to stop gunboats moving on the Mississippi?

"Up here," came Bullock's bass voice. "We got a real good view from here."

Slocum's horse slipped and slid along the muddy bank of the levee. He finally dismounted and led the horse to the top. By the time he arrived, Jessica and the other three were already dismounted and staring out across the dark, sluggishly moving river.

"There, John? You see it?"

He made out the shape of a gunboat steaming toward shore. It would put into the docks in New Orleans in a few minutes. Once it was in command of the riverfront, other ships laden with troops could come down the river from Baton Rouge and other posts within days. McMullan's victory would be short-lived.

"You still don't appreciate the planning that went into the filibuster," Jessica chided.

"Those mountain howitzers might be good for blowing up trains at point-blank range, but they can't reach to the middle of the Mississippi with any accuracy. The gunboat has artillery that can reach all the way to shore."

"That's true," Jessica said. "But they don't understand what we have been doing for the past twelve hours."

The explosion rocked Slocum back. In the middle of the river rose a spout of dark water and brilliant, eye-dazzling flame. He saw the gunboat outlined for the briefest instant. It seemed to rise on its haunches like some wounded beast, but when it settled back down it kept sinking. Nose-first, it vanished into the river. In seconds it was gone.

"That was an armor-plated boat," he said. "What happened?"

"Torpedoes. We laid out torpedoes and the gunboat crossed one, detonating it," Jessica said with some pride. "Griggs is so smart!"

"That was his idea?" Somehow Slocum didn't doubt it. Braxton Griggs struck him as a bitter man who spent his days loathing everything and everyone that had blinded him. He'd never been a merciful man, and underwater torpedoes would seem the perfect weapon to him.

"Another boat," called Bullock. "It's streaming straight at us."

"Open fire on it," Jessica said calmly.

"With what?" asked Slocum, but again there was much the woman had not shared with him. The levee quaked under his feet as a heavy cannon belched flame and iron ball from near the shoreline. The artillerist had misjudged the range. The cannonball flew high over the second gunboat.

"The boat's comin' round!" Bullock cried. "Take cover. She's gonna fire on us!"

The words weren't out of his mouth when two long tongues of orange and yellow flamed licked toward the levee. One shell went wide. The other crashed into the levee just under Slocum's feet. He felt himself flying backward through the air, aware of the precipitous flight heels over head, and yet curiously detached from the death closing in all around him.

16

Slocum sputtered and spat mud. He struggled about, floundering in water rising around him. He finally sat up. His head felt as if someone had put it inside a drum, then played a march for the entire Union army to pass by in parade.

"John, hurry. We must get out of here."

"What happened?" he asked, still stunned by his flight off the top of the levee. He stared up the muddy slope and saw the sluggish water of the Mississippi River forcing its way across the top of the dirt mound. "The cannon went off and the gunship returned fire," he said, pieces falling together.

"We were blown off the top of the levee, John. Now come on!" Jessica tugged insistently on his arm and got him to his feet. He stumbled along until his strength returned.

"Where are the others? Bullock?"

"Dead, gone, the gunship was too accurate. It is heading for the New Orleans docks. We need to get the money for the gems now."

"What?" Slocum's head still hummed as if a beehive had been shoved into his skull. "The diamonds and emeralds?"

161

"Yes, John, yes, yes. We need to take care of that now."

Her urgency caused Slocum's thoughts to go down a different track. Jessica wasn't saying anything about warning Frank McMullan. All she wanted now was the money Slocum had promised for the precious stones.

"We need to let the general know the gunship got through," he said. "If they land marines behind his lines, he'll find himself caught between troops on the trains and those moving in from the docks."

"I'll send word. Now let's get the money. We are going to need it fast for the filibuster."

Slocum and Jessica found horses and rode in silence. He let her take the lead, and didn't even try to keep even with her. His entire body ached, and he only now began to think straight. Nothing was going the way he thought it might. The death of Bullock and the two others with Jessica had been so sudden. It was as if a single fusillade had changed McMullan's fortune—and Jessica's. Somehow, their two futures were not as intertwined as Slocum had thought earlier.

"I buried the stones out in the swamp, near the camp where you trained the artillerists," she said.

"You did?"

"I am treasurer of the New South," Jessica explained too quickly. "It is my duty to be sure there is cash enough to finance the revolt. We must get more men, pay the ones who are so gallantly battling."

"What's my pay as a captain?" he asked.

This rocked Jessica, but just for a moment. She smiled her sly smile and said, "Wealth and power—and more—beyond your dreams. Now hurry." She urged her horse through the winding path, missing boggy patches, until they arrived at the bivouac. McMullan's troopers had already abandoned the site. Slocum pictured them huddled near railroad tracks, taking potshots at Yankee soldiers trying vainly to get through their blockade to New Orleans.

The woman dismounted and hurried to a banyan tree with tangled roots. She dug like a ferret, throwing dirt in all directions. She tugged and pulled and finally came up with a chamois bag like the one Slocum had carried the emeralds in.

"Now, let's get the money and—"

"We'll have to get McMullan," said Slocum. "The fence wants to deal only with the top dog. It's his way of assuring his safety."

"But how? The fewer people involved, the better for us all."

"He wants to meet McMullan. Is that a problem?"

Jessica paused far too long. Slocum saw the way her face screwed up in deep thought. She finally tucked the bag of gems into her bodice, wiggled delightfully, then went to her horse and mounted.

"We can find McMullan in Banks' Arcade on Magazine Street. That's his headquarters. He has couriers running out to each of the detachments."

"He's in real danger then," Slocum said. "That's not far from the docks where the gunship is heading." He knew the ship, unless it had run afoul of another of the torpedoes Jessica had ordered laid out in the river, had already reached the crescent bend in the river and steamed down to the city. Jessica's reluctance to involve McMullan in the exchange for the gems puzzled Slocum. He was missing something.

"We can get there in less than an hour if we kill the horses," she said. And ride like the wind they did. Jessica's horse survived, but it was worthless by the time they reached McMullan's headquarters. Slocum's died under him a few blocks down the street from the three-story building. Jessica left him to make his way on his own, and rode ahead.

He hiked up, still aching and bone tired from all he had

been through as Jessica's horse weakly staggered away, heading for a water barrel. The woman had already gone into the filibusterer's headquarters.

Slocum hastened after her, reaching Jessica and McMullan in time for the woman to whirl about and grab for his arm.

"Do we have to take him, John? The blue-bellies are marching up from the docks. Another gunship from the Gulf arrived. We hadn't known about it."

"What's this mysterious rendezvous you arranged, Captain?" asked McMullan. "Will it really help turn the tide? We've lost half our men. The other half are fighting for their lives."

Slocum knew then that Jessica had not told McMullan the reason for the meeting. She was playing her own game, and it was independent of the would-be liberator of New Orleans. None of her machinations mattered to Slocum now. He wanted to get McMullan into Devereau's presence so the jeweler could identify the man who had killed his daughter.

Slocum would carry out the death sentence. But he had to be sure. He wanted Devereau to know justice had been served. Even more, he wanted McMullan to know why he died.

Then there was the matter of the precious gems secreted in Jessica's ample bodice.

Pierre Devereau stood to bring his daughter's killer to justice *and* get back his stolen property.

"This man you're taking us to, Captain Slocum. Can he really field an army?"

"General, please, there is so little time," Jessica said, interposing herself between McMullan and Slocum. "You are needed if we are to save the day."

"Yes, yes, I see that." McMullan coughed harshly and wiped sweat from his pale face. Slocum thought the man might keel over, but some inner force kept him moving.

He looked at Jessica, but the woman refused to meet his gaze.

"There are horses out back," Jessica said. "We can get to Slocum's ally and be back in the fight by dawn."

"A counterattack," McMullan said in a strong, booming voice. "That's what we need. Another thousand men will turn those blue bastards out of New Orleans once and for all."

"For the cause," Jessica murmured, but it carried no conviction.

Slocum started to mount when they found the horses in back of Banks' Arcade, then stopped when he saw the trouble McMullan was having. He boosted the man into the saddle. McMullan looked down, but his eyes were glazed as if by fever. He stared at Slocum dully, his vision never quite focusing. What he saw was not apparent.

"This way, General. Hurry, hurry," urged Jessica. She took the reins to McMullan's horse and tugged gently, getting the horse walking. Slocum mounted and led the way directly to Devereau's house. They saw occasional army patrols along the streets, but they were not stopped. The soldiers moved with determined steps, going to seize strategic points throughout the city. Whatever chance McMullan might have had to wrest New Orleans from the Union had passed quickly, Slocum saw.

Slocum watched Frank McMullan wobble in the saddle as they approached Devereau's house. He put his heels into his horse's flanks to catch up with the general and keep him from toppling. Sweat poured down the man's face, and his eyes had a sunken, dead look to them.

"Why are we coming here?" demanded Jessica. She looked about, growing increasingly frantic by the moment.

"What's wrong with him?" Slocum asked. "He looks half past dead."

"It's the jungle fever. It's come back."

"Malaria?" Slocum asked, recoiling from McMullan.

He had heard it didn't pass from one man to another, that foul air was responsible. He wasn't sure how the disease spread, but he wasn't going to take any chances.

"Might be. He contracted just about every tropical disease known down in that hellhole of Sao Lourenço," Jessica said with stinging bitterness.

"Captain, we must retreat," McMullan said. "The attack has to be put off. For a while. Until we regroup."

Slocum thought it was the disease eating at McMullan's mind and body, until he looked past the man and saw a squad of Yankee soldiers marching down the road in front of Devereau's house. They had bayonets fixed, and their determined pace showed they had found their quarry. They came directly for McMullan, Jessica, and Slocum.

"We've got to get out of here. There's no way we can answer their questions, if they even bother to ask any," Jessica said.

Slocum had to agree. The grim expressions on these soldiers' faces told him they were more likely to shoot or stab first than ask questions. That McMullan wore the gray uniform of a Confederate cavalry officer would not sit well with any of the soldiers.

"This way," Slocum said, wheeling his horse down a side street. They galloped along to avoid the troopers, Slocum cursing his bad luck. Another few minutes and he would have had McMullan in Devereau's presence and the entire sorry affair laid to rest—along with Frank McMullan's bones.

Slocum frowned when that thought crossed his mind. Something about a cemetery pricked his memory but he couldn't—quite—put it into words. Then they were dodging rifle fire from the squad following them. The sergeant in charge had decided they were suspicious and had ordered his men to open fire.

"This way, down toward the river," cried Slocum. "We can reach the warehouse and—"

"There's nothing left in it," Jessica said. "All the ord-nance got moved out."

"I don't have the ammo for much of a fight," Slocum said.

"I know where we can take shelter, at least for a while. Ride like you mean it, John. And don't let that fool fall out of the saddle. We can still use him," she shot back, glaring at Frank McMullan.

McMullan rode mechanically, staying in the addle more through inertia than any intent. Slocum followed Jessica until it was too late.

She rode into the wood yard at the end of Elysian Fields Street—and had already dickered with the Live Oak Boys by the time Slocum and McMullan came up.

It was too late to run. Slocum could only bluff now.

17

Slocum pulled back, then decided to bluff it out. He wasn't sure if any of the Live Oak Boys knew of his prior excursion into their camp or who had killed Gus and the sentries. Then Slocum tensed a little. Street swaggered into view. This was the man responsible for Texas Jack's death.

Slocum remembered Gus's last words before he had fallen to his death. Gus had declared that Street didn't have the emeralds they had stolen. They had been turned over to . . . the person hiring the Live Oak Boys to rob the couriers.

He turned in the saddle and stared at Jessica. She had the emeralds, as well as the diamonds stolen from Devereau's shop. They hadn't ridden into a viper's den. Or rather, they had, and it was *Jessica's* den of pet vipers. She had ordered the Live Oak Boys after the emeralds.

"Good to see you again, little lady," Street said. The burly Live Oak Boy reached up to help her down. Jessica ignored him, slipping her leg over the saddle and dropping to the ground without his help. She turned and glared at him.

"We need help, Street. We need men to help pull our fat out of the fire."

"Heard the gunshots. Sounds like half the damn city is at war. That fancy-ass dude back there your general?" Street pointed at McMullan and laughed. Slocum wanted to throw down on the gang member and rob him of life as he had done to Texas Jack. But he held back. Too much swirled around him that he did not understand.

"You mean for me and the boys to go pound on Yankee skulls?" Street asked. "Hell, we done that during the war, a lot of us."

Slocum doubted that any of these men had ever been in the CSA—or any army. They were too undisciplined, and lived forever in contempt of authority. Not that Slocum had much loyalty left after seeing how things had had worked in New Orleans and elsewhere because of Reconstruction and the thieving carpetbaggers.

"But we can't take time out from our busy jobs, not right now," Street said, canting his head to one side and eyeing Jessica. "Course yer personal attention might change my mind."

Slocum never saw Jessica move. All that appeared to happen was Street standing a little straighter.

"Don't ever suggest that, you filthy pig," Jessica said. "I am a lady, a lady of the New South."

Street started to tremble. Slocum saw how Jessica had grabbed him. The Live Oak Boy might have broken the painful grip on his privates since he was so much stronger. But he would have died with a derringer slug in his heart if he had tried.

"Whatever you say," Street muttered. He heaved a sigh of relief as Jessica released him and lowered her derringer.

"Now," she said almost primly. "How many men can you get into the field to support the valiant soldiers of the New Confederacy?"

"For the cause?" Street grated out in a sarcastic drawl, getting back some of his bravado. "None, if we don't get paid real good for it. This ain't our fight."

"You can make it yours," Jessica said.

Slocum saw that McMullan struggled to keep up with the conversation. The sweat beading his forehead earlier had evaporated, even in the dampness of the New Orleans night. But McMullan had turned a pasty color that spoke volumes of how sick the man was. Slocum wondered if the fever eating at his body might not also have affected his brain. It had seemed that only a crazy man would launch a war against the entire might of the United States. Even with a hundred times the equipment and men, McMullan's filibuster had no chance of succeeding.

"For a price it can be our fight," Street said firmly. "You're askin' us to get shot up by Yankees who'd like nothin' better than to kill a true patriotic Southerner."

"So your patriotism can be bought?" she said, losing her temper.

Street didn't back down this time.

"Reckon that sums it up real good," the Live Oak Boy said. He thrust out his jaw belligerently, then looked around to see if the other Live Oak Boys approved. They did.

"Ten dollars each," Jessica said.

"Fifty. And there'll be a hundred of us. We'll fight like a thousand men, so's you'll be gettin' a real bargain. We'll burn this town to the ground, won't we, boys?"

A roar went up. Slocum's hand moved to his six-shooter when he saw more of the gang drifting in from their camp in the middle of the wood yard. There just might be a hundred of them.

There were a hundred Live Oak Boys—and Jessica needed five thousand dollars to pay them off.

"I'll get you the money," she said. "Get ready to attack at dawn."

"Not much time," observed Street. "That's not more 'n a couple hours from now."

"Get your men over to Banks' Arcade," Jessica said. "I'll have the money for you as soon as I can fetch it."

She came over to where McMullan sat astride his horse, looking confused. Her green and blue eyes turned up to the general. "Frank. Frank! General McMullan!"

"What? Can we launch a counterattack?"

"You'll have to lead the troops, General," Jessica said. Slocum did not point out McMullan was in no condition to lead schoolchildren from a classroom. "We'll get the money, and the Live Oak Boys will back up our brave soldiers. You can ride at the head of their regiment and win the battle."

"The filibuster will succeed," McMullan said, color coming into his cheeks. He struck a pose that looked military.

"Get on back to Banks' Arcade," Jessica said. "You know the way. Can you make it, General?"

"I will triumph."

Slocum watched the befuddled filibusterer ride off, swaying slightly in the saddle. Whatever tropical diseases ravaged him had finally conquered Frank McMullan. He might make it to the Magazine Street headquarters, but leading troops in combat against trained soldiers was out of the question.

"He's not going to make it," Slocum said. "I'll go get him and—"

"No," Jessica said. She drew her derringer and pointed it at him. "You'll come with me."

Slocum looked from the small gun to the Live Oak Boys, and finally at the rapidly vanishing Frank Mc-Mullan. He wasn't going to be able to drag McMullan to Devereau's house so the jeweler could identify him. If Slocum didn't do something fast, McMullan might die on his own, cheating Slocum of his revenge. That McMullan would die was certain. Slocum wanted the death to avenge Claudine's murder, and not come at the hand of some nameless damn Yankee just following orders.

"Don't cross me, John," Jessica said in a voice that brooked no argument. "We will get Griggs and then see if your fence is willing to pay for these jewels." She patted her bodice where the small bag of gems still rested.

"Why fetch Griggs?"

Jessica mounted, keeping the derringer in her hand. Slocum might have tried galloping off, but she was good enough a shot to hit either him or his horse. Falling to the ground this close to the Live Oak Boys' hideout would have spelled his death.

Slocum felt so many threads slipping through his fingers. McMullan was returning to Banks' Arcade, out of reach. Street was whipping his gang into a fighting frenzy, and Slocum could not bring him to justice for killing Texas Jack. And now Jessica was insisting on going to Devereau in the mistaken belief he could give her money to pay the Live Oak Boys for their fight against the Union soldiers.

They rode off, Jessica guiding him through the maze of narrow alleys until they came to a small house off Girod Street.

"Griggs!" she shouted. "We've got to go. Now!"

The blind man came out, feeling his way. He used a cane to guide himself through the maze of debris in the street. As if he had done it a thousand times, he climbed into the saddle behind Jessica.

"Ride, John. We have so little time."

Slocum rode in silence, his mind racing to churn up a plan of action. Here and there in the distance he saw the blue-jacketed soldiers setting up control posts at major intersections. Nothing had suggested itself to him by the time they reached Devereau's house. Jessica looked across the street at the burned shop, but said nothing. Braxton Griggs dismounted and followed them to the front door.

"Are you crossing me, John?" she asked.

"Why do you keep asking that?"

"Because you're a no-account snake, that's why," said Braxton Griggs. "You might have her fooled, but not me, Slocum. You left me for dead. You—"

Griggs broke off his tirade when Pierre Devereau opened the door. At first he saw only Slocum. Then he looked past and saw Jessica. The Frenchman's eyes went wide.

"Her!" he cried, his face turning livid. "She's the one who killed my Claudine!"

Slocum wasn't sure who was more startled at the accusation, him or Jessica.

18

"You killed her! I saw you!" Devereau lurched forward, his thin arm coming up over his head. Slocum thought the jeweler meant to punch Jessica, then saw the deadly flash of the blade of a silvery knife the man had picked up from a table just inside the door.

Jessica fired point-blank into Devereau's chest. The small Frenchman staggered but kept coming, intense, all-consuming anger driving him. Jessica fired a second time and missed. Pierre Devereau did not. His knife drove down into Jessica's breast, killing her instantly.

"What's happening? Why did you shoot, Jess?" cried Braxton Griggs. "Jess! Jess! What's wrong? Answer me." Griggs blundered about until he discovered the woman's body. "It's you, ain't it, Slocum? You did this, you dirty double-dealing snake!" The cane in the blind man's hand separated into a sheath and a wicked silver sword blade. Griggs lunged forward awkwardly. The man missed Slocum by a country mile.

"What are you getting so worked up for, Griggs?" asked Slocum, backing away. He had to get to Devereau. The man lay on the ground, bleeding from a chest wound.

"She was my daughter, damn you!" Griggs slashed at thin air again.

From where he lay sprawled on his own doorstep, Devereau spat blood and called out angrily, "And Claudine was *my* daughter. She killed her. I saw her kill my dear Claudine!"

Slocum moved fast when he saw how Griggs homed in on Devereau's voice. The sword cane aimed straight for Devereau's face. The former guerrilla lunged just as Slocum drew and squeezed off a round from his Colt. The well-aimed bullet took Griggs in the right side of the head, knocking him away from the fallen jeweler. Griggs's lunge went wild and missed Devereau by inches.

Slocum found himself panting harshly and his heart hammering. He had shot Braxton Griggs in the head, in the same place a sniper bullet had taken the man during the war. The difference now was obvious. Griggs was dead this time.

"Devereau, take it easy. Don't try to get up."

"Slocum! She killed my darling. I saw her. She did it, she did it." Tears ran down the man's cheeks. Slocum cradled the jeweler's head in his lap. Devereau looked up at him with forlorn eyes. Bubbly pink froth choked him. Slocum knew then that Pierre Devereau was a goner. Jessica's bullet had punctured a lung. The Frenchman was slowly drowning in his own blood, and there was nothing Slocum or anyone this side of heaven could do about it.

"Her name was Jessica," Slocum said. "Jessica Griggs. I think she was looting in the name of McMullan's filibuster and keeping it. She and her father were stealing from a man too sick to know what was going on." He finally realized it had not been McMullan he had seen in the cemetery before O'Leary was killed. It had been Jessica—and her father, Braxton Griggs.

Slocum didn't know whether to pity or loathe them. Then he remembered all the evil Braxton Griggs had done during the war. Blind or with hawk-sharp vision, he had been a despicable killer. And his daughter had been stealing from a man following a star, no matter how deranged that had been on McMullan's part.

"Mr. Slocum, there's something I did not tell."

"There's a lot you didn't tell me," Slocum said, "but Claudine's killer has paid for it, and I got back your diamonds. And the emeralds too."

"No, no, not that. Forget the stones. I will never need them."

"I'll see your friend gets them back then," Slocum said.

"He was dying. My dear friend Leclerc. He wanted to see . . ." Devereau coughed again, visibly weakening. "He is gone by now, and soon I will join him. And Claudine."

"Take it easy," Slocum said. "Claudine's killer is rotting in Hell by now."

"*Non, non!* I must confess. I . . . I started the fire. It was an accident. I carried a lamp when I heard something in the shop. We grappled, that awful woman and I. I did not have the courage to go into the back of the shop to save Claudine or you when I dropped the lamp and the fire was everywhere!"

"There was nothing you could do. Claudine was dead before the fire started," Slocum said, trying to ease the pain for the man. He didn't know if he succeeded. Pierre Devereau had died.

Slocum slid Devereau's head to the ground as gently as he could and looked around at the minor carnage on the man's doorstep. It had taken decades to remove Braxton Griggs from the earth. The entire Federal army had failed. He had obviously lived in dangerous Brazilian jungles with his daughter and survived. And then Griggs had come to New Orleans to plunder—and die. Slocum felt no thrill in being present when it happened. And he had mixed feelings about Jessica's death. She had killed Claudine and stolen from Devereau everything he held dearest, but Slocum had been attracted to her like a moth to a flame.

"Burn in Hell," Slocum decided. He reached over and fumbled in Jessica's bodice. Robbing the dead didn't sit well with him, but then Jessica had been a murderer and a thief. The small chamois bag tumbled out. Slocum tucked it into his pocket and stood. A deep breath did little to settle his nerves.

Gunfire echoed along the streets, reminding Slocum he still had some scores to settle. McMullan seemed an innocent enough dupe, except that he intended to lead other men who were more patriotic than sensible.

But Street . . .

Slocum had a score to settle with the Live Oak Boy over Texas Jack Bennon's death. Then he would be square and could get the hell out of New Orleans.

It took a few minutes for Slocum to be sure he had enough armament to take on Street and any of the Live Oak Boys with him. Two rifles fitted snugly into the scabbard on his saddle. He had a second six-shooter tucked into his belt, taken from Jessica's saddlebags. She had ridden forth with a small arsenal.

And the bag of precious stones weighed him down as if they had turned to lead. Dead man's stones.

He touched them, made a promise to Claudine and her father that they would be taken care of properly, then set off at a gallop in the direction of McMullan's headquarters. Before he had gone a quarter mile he found himself having to dodge army patrols and barricades. More than one intersection had a squad armed with rifles and fixed bayonets searching everyone passing through. Slocum saw enough scruffy derelicts being herded off to jail to know the soldiers were serious about being certain of anyone they checked.

He wouldn't stand a chance in a million of bluffing his way past the guards. As a result it took him almost an hour to go less than two miles, but he did it without running afoul of the troopers.

Slocum dismounted a block away from Banks' Arcade. Dawn sent pink fingers over the horizon, and silvery glints off the glass in the building. He advanced cautiously, wondering if the soldiers had laid a trap for any of the filibusterers eluding them around town.

The army seemed oblivious to McMullan's headquarters.

Loud voices from down Magazine Street sent Slocum scurrying for cover. He dived behind a pile of rotting garbage, and held his breath as Street and a score of Live Oak Boys swaggered past. They were armed to the teeth. A few carried shotguns, others sported rifles, and the ones with pistols stuck into their belts swung their wooden staves in whistling oaken arcs.

"Where do we fight, Street?" asked a bruiser half again the size of their leader. "I want to bust some heads."

"We wait here a spell," Street said. "We don't get ourselves involved 'less they come through with the money."

Slocum cursed when the Live Oak Boys started milling around outside the front entrance to the Arcade. He wiggled on his belly and reached an alley that led around to the rear. Halfway down the alley he heard sounds at the rear of the building. Slocum advanced more carefully, pressing against the wall and peering around the corner.

Colonel Demeter and upward of fifty bloodied and powder-singed men filed through the rear door into Banks' Arcade.

It didn't take a genius to figure out the colonel had been soundly whipped in battle and these few men were all that remained of McMullan's filibuster.

"There they are!" came a cry from some distance. Ragged rifle fire echoed as the whine of bullets cut through the air in front of Slocum. One bullet caught Demeter and spun him around. The would-be colonel fell to his knees. From somewhere he drew out a sword and lifted it.

"Rally to me, men! Attack!"

Slocum was startled to see that many of the men who had filed into the Arcade now piled back out. They fired wildly at the Yankee soldiers. Slocum realized he was going to be caught in the middle of a fight unless he retreated.

"Charge!" cried Demeter. The white-haired man struggled to his feet and stumbled along, waving his saber around and dragging his injured leg behind. Slocum saw Demeter pass the mouth of the alley where he watched in growing horror.

Those supporting Demeter ran forward, but with every step they took, there were fewer of them. The trained soldiers held their ground. The bluecoat sergeant kept them firing in a steady withering barrage that took more and more out of the fight.

Somehow, Demeter remained standing. Slocum watched in fascination as the man slashed at one soldier. The young bluecoat private ducked, then lunged forward, his bayonet entering Demeter's belly. The blood-drenched tip poked out Demeter's back. For a moment, the tableau burned itself indelibly into Slocum's brain, rivaling the look on Devereau's face at seeing Jessica's corpse stretched out on the street.

The soldier fired his rifle, sending Demeter staggering away to fall flat on his back. His saber clattered to the ground. All that remained was the stench of gun smoke and blood.

"There, there they are! They have killed our valiant hero!" came a strong voice.

"Get back, you fool!" cried Slocum. McMullan emerged from the rear door, accompanied by the remainder of the men who had arrived with Demeter. "They'll cut you down!"

McMullan either didn't hear or ignored Slocum's warn-

ing. He drew his six-shooter and began firing. The ragtag
band with him hesitated, then joined the battle. In spite
of his misgivings, Slocum had to admit blind heroism
sometimes outdid discipline. The Yankee sergeant ordered
his men to retreat, giving McMullan the brief victory.

"We will take New Orleans!" cried McMullan. Slocum saw the fever burning again in the man's wild eyes.
He might not even know what he was doing. The thought
of returning to the land of his birth and leaving behind
Sao Lourenço and all the hardship in the renegade colony
drove Frank McMullan more than good sense now.

The rattle of heavy caissons alerted Slocum to new
danger. He didn't wait to see what threat McMullan
faced. The filibusterer tried to form up his remaining recruits. The Gatling gun rattling out leaden death cut
through McMullan and his men like a scythe cutting win-
ter wheat. McMullan gamboled wildly about in a death
dance, heavy leaden slugs ripping through his diseased
body. Then he collapsed and so did his rebellion.

The New Orleans filibuster was at an end.

Slocum hurried back up the alley and onto Magazine
Street. He stopped dead in his tracks when he saw Street
and a half-dozen of his cronies standing in a tight circling
arguing.

"We kin steal ever'thing in the building, I tell you,"
shouted Street.

"It's too dangerous," protested another of the Live
Oak Boys. "The army! They're everywhere!"

The Live Oak Boy protesting his leader's orders to loot
Banks' Arcade clamped his mouth shut and stared straight
at Slocum. Then Hell broke loose from a half-dozen directions.

From either end of Magazine Street came shots. The
army had circled McMullan's headquarters, and now considered anyone near it to be the enemy. Two of Street's
gang members slumped to the ground, riddled with bullets.
Two others yelped when they sustained minor wounds. But

in the middle of it all stood Slocum and Street, as if a bubble had formed over them and held out the world.

"You killed my friend," Slocum said. Street's expression went from confusion to pure rage. Slocum doubted Street even knew who Slocum meant. Street had killed too many men to ever remember or learn their names.

Street growled deep in his throat and whipped out a six-gun shoved into his waistband.

He was too slow by a heartbeat. Slocum drew and fired. Street's muscles refused to believe he had died. The six-shooter came out. Slocum drilled him again and again. The Live Oak Boy's gun discharged into the ground, then the hand holding the six-shooter relaxed in death. Slocum got off two more shots before Street hit the ground.

Then the bubble burst. All had been silence for Slocum up to that point. Now he heard loud cries of fury and fear. Rifles cracked. Slugs raced past him. And the remaining Live Oak Boys threw down their rifles and bellowed for mercy.

Slocum glanced behind him. Coming up the alley where he had watched McMullan's last stand was a squad of Yankee soldiers with their bayonets lowered and ready for blood. To run into the Arcade would be a mistake. Slocum bolted, vaulting over Street's body and putting his head down. A few shots came his way, but they missed. That was good enough.

Slocum slammed into a brick wall, bounced off it, and sprinted through a door into a building. He ran down the long, narrow hallway, seeing he had burst into a brothel. The women in the cribs looked up sleepily at him. It was too late for a customer. It was too early for their pimp to bother them.

One or two threw garbage at him, and then Slocum was out the back way. He found a horse three blocks away and stole it. In ten minutes he was a half mile from Banks' Arcade and the horrific death scene there. In twenty, he rode along the levee heading south toward where Andy Jackson had whipped the British seventy-five years earlier. Only when Slocum thought he had gone far enough to leave all the confusion and carnage behind him in New Orleans did he rein back.

The Mississippi rolled by, unperturbed by all the killing upriver. In its muddy flow he saw both serenity and a power that could never be denied.

He reached into his pocket and pulled out the chamois bag. He opened it. Out poured the diamonds taken when Claudine was killed and the emeralds he and Texas Jack had lost to the Live Oak Boys.

"There's too much blood on these," he said. He dropped the chamois bag to the muddy track on the top of the levee. Then he threw all the emeralds and all but one of the diamonds into the Mississippi. It seemed fitting to him.

The single diamond he had kept he held up to catch the morning light. For a moment he thought he saw Claudine's smiling, lovely face reflected in its many facets. Then a cloud crossed the sun and the brightness faded. He tucked the diamond into his shirt pocket as a keepsake to always remind him of Claudine and her father.

He rode on south, intending to cross the river somewhere nearer the Gulf. In a few days he could be in Texas, and in a month, California. Slocum would have to decide then if even the Pacific Coast was far enough away.

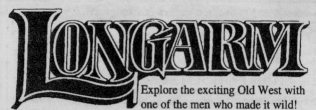

LONGARM

Explore the exciting Old West with
one of the men who made it wild!